T0006089

BRYHER

BEOWULF

A NOVEL

SCHAFFNER PRESS
TUCSON, ARIZONA

to
SYLVIA BEACH
and the memory of
ADRIENNE MONNIER

INTRODUCTION
"COMRADE BULLDOG AMONG THE RUINS"

"Two wars in a single generation asked too much of any race."
–Beowulf

WHO OR WHAT IS "Beowulf," the title of a book chronicling the Blitz? Moreover, who is this writer? Primarily an historical novelist, Bryher (1894–1983), little known today, her writings largely out of print,[1] was a pioneer, a model of personal and cultural defiance. Before World War II, she published among other works, two volumes of poetry, two early coming-of-age memoirs, *Development* (1920) and *Two Selves* (1923)—both early accounts of gender dysphoria in modern literary history. Bryher was a woman, but felt like a boy, as she claimed, from infancy.

"Comrade Bulldog" was Bryher's working title for her first novel that she later renamed *Beowulf*, taking the same title of the Anglo-Saxon foundational poem from the early 10th century, recorded by an anonymous scribe, long before England existed and half a millennium before the Empire was born. Beowulf, the armored hero of the ancient epic, travels from Geatland—what is now Sweden—to assist the Danes in combating the monster Grendel, and Grendel's mother. While successful in fending them off, his old age (fifty!) presents another challenge, a dragon, terrorizing his subjects; he slays it, though mortally wounded as a result.

In this hybrid docu-novel, Bryher has morphed Beowulf into a bulldog, a miniaturized plaster statuette, a popular mascot to decorate a teashop. Known as "The Warming Pan," this establishment became the pivotal locale of her novel, based on an actual tearoom run by a pair of women. As Bryher describes: "Selina and Angelina supplied their clients with soup, meat, two veg and dessert for two shillings and ninepence. They were country people, they bought all the ingredients they could from farms and the cooking was plain but excellent. Such places are now extinct. I liked it because, as I said, I could go there without fear. There was a large notice, *Dogs Welcome*, hanging on the door and as I am to those, but only those, who know me intimately, Fido, I felt at ease and knew that I should not be hustled out."[2]

Using the fusty classic's title was her joke with legend; her bulldog is humanity's finest. By the end of the novel, it seems we are all plaster—when those staying near the City faced total annihilation (one rumor had it that London could be demolished in three years). Bryher probably foresaw that, although Britain was wholly unprepared for World War II, its bulldog spirit would triumph in the end. However, as in legend, the first battle waged and won, like the Great War, the second amounted to a muted victory, in which the victor prevails, though mortally wounded. We are not supermen or superwomen, Bryher seems to be telling us, nor could she idealize England's own eroding Empire that had sustained the

Victorian-era sense of solid well-being.

Beowulf was actually the first of Bryher's eight novels, that received critical acclaim in the 1950s and 1960's. Instead of attending to the heroic, she focused upon the lives of ordinary citizens as shaped or disfigured by their rulers. She put it starkly: "there would be a gulf between the bombed and the unraided."

Bryher was allergic to nationalism of any stripe—an obsession ignited when she was five, when, visiting the 1900 World Exhibition in Paris, she recognized that the Boer war made the French disdain the English; at first she wanted to put up fisticuffs, but was disarmed when she learned the French shared her values of *égalité, fraternité, liberté*.[3] These words entranced Bryher—ultimately leading to *Beowulf.* But to understand her engagement with history, and her first book that confronts the daily reality of London during World War II, the reader needs some familiarity with Bryher's own history— and her most significant and enduring love relationship with the imagist poet H.D.

———

Bryher was born Annie Winifred Ellerman, on September 2, 1894 to the then-unwed couple, John Ellerman and Hannah Glover. Her father had made a fortune in shipping and other enterprises, and upon his death in 1933 was said to have been the richest man in England. The constraints of the Victorian age made her wonder "if adventure had died just before I was born," which propelled her to conclude that "if I wanted to be happy when I grew up I had to become a cabin boy and run away from the inexplicable taboos of Victorian life."[4]

At an early age, she secretly sensed what Havelock Ellis, the sexologist, later confirmed in 1919 that she was "a girl only by accident."⁵

During her early years, Bryher travelled extensively with her parents, spending winters in Italy, Egypt, Greece, and the south of France, and summers in Switzerland. The family spent little time in Britain. Travel advanced Ellerman's shipping business, and fulfilled his desire to escape snobbery and restraint. During these early treks, Bryher learned Arabic, tried to decipher hieroglyphics, rode her first camel, learned to barter, and traded thoughts with Sufis. At twelve, she had a vision near the wall of Euryelus, the ancient fortress at Syracuse, where, according to mythic lore, one's fate is sealed: "seized by the throat, barely able to breathe," she was hit with "a terrifying sense of ecstasy," and understood with undeniable certainty that Clio, muse of history, was destined to be her life's mistress: to "write of things was to become part of them. It was to see *before* the beginning and *after* the end. I almost screamed against the pain of the moment that from its very intensity could not last."⁶ Close study of the past helped her to view history as non-linear and see beyond it and the present, as captured in this assertion in *Beowulf*: "the distant thuddings of the mobile guns were the footsteps of mammoths."

In 1909, when Bryher was 15, her mother gave birth to a boy, John Jr. Her father, knighted for his help in the Boer War, purchased a mansion in Mayfair, 1 South Audley Street, close to Hyde Park and adjacent to the Dorchester Hotel. Under English law, their newborn was also destined to be illegitimate; thus Bryher's parents snuck off to obtain a "Scotch Marriage." Bryher's childhood utopia came to an abrupt close with her brother's birth. Her parents shifted their fantasies to John Jr.'s future, throwing the teenage Bryher into paroxysms, not only of anger, but despair. Increasingly, Bryher disappointed her mother's expectations that she would develop into a "lady." (She puts it for one of her *Beowulf* characters: "everything should have been so different if she had been a man.") As a child, it was easier to maintain the fantasy of boyhood. One of the family's guests criticized Bryher as not "quite normal," advising they put her in school "to knock the edges off."[7] Much to her horror, they followed this suggestion, enrolling her at Queenswood Boarding School, twenty miles outside London, as a day-student.

During this period, she began calling herself Bryher after the wildest island in The Scillies, off the coast of Cornwall. Fiercely independent, she wanted to make her way without the assistance of her father's surname. After Queenswood, Bryher returned to Audley Street, and spent the First World War studying in her father's library, attempting to write, and meet poets. She corresponded with the American poet, Amy Lowell, who was friends with a number of Imagist poets, including H.D., born Hilda Doolitttle in Bethlehem, Pennsylvania on September 10, 1886. Hilda had followed her one-time suitor, Ezra Pound, to Europe. Through Pound, H.D. met and married Richard Aldington. Through Lowell, Bryher discovered H.D., deeply moved by her debut collection, *Sea Garden* (1916).

The couple's forty-two-year, intimate, tumultuous yet productive relationship began as World War I ended, and would continue on to H.D.'s death in 1961. At the time of their meeting, Aldington, H.D.'s soldier husband, was embroiled in a blatant adulterous affair, leading her to escape to Cornwall at the invitation of the Scottish music critic and composer Cecil Gray. With her photographic memory, Bryher memorized all of H.D.'s poems, and descended upon her there on July 17, 1918. H.D. was fascinated with this amorphously-gendered being. The H.D. and Bryher saga felt destined by both women. While sometimes maintaining separate households, they remained discretely together, corresponding when apart nearly daily. H.D. wrote "Remember that it all began with a bluuue swalllllow and you—"[8] As a result of her tryst with Cecil Gray, H.D. was now pregnant with Perdita ("Pup"), and meeting Bryher felt like rebirth. Now separated from Richard Aldington, H.D. committed perjury and registered Perdita as his, only to fear he would unveil her and Bryher's unusual state of affairs— two mothers and a baby.

An unusual couple, Bryher was five feet, next to the very tall H.D.; Bryher's smallness, H.D. observed, made her like a literary Brueghel, who is said to have put his diminutive size to advantage by doing sketches under a table, invisible to those unobserved.

———

H.D. and Bryher explored the physical realms of Cornwall, Greece, Egypt, and aesthetic and intellectual worlds, too, in their mutual fascination with cinema and psychoanalysis. They shared visions in Corfu, cultivating a telepathic form of communication. Their birthdates separated by eight days and eight years, they celebrated the "octave" together. But they moved cautiously into the unknown realm of their relationship: one a bisexual, the other proto-transgender. Bryher's parents, particularly her mother, kept her pinned to her shawl. The couple finessed their relationship by burying it in plain sight. Bryher asserted her freedom by marrying Robert McAlmon in 1920 on her trip to United States with H.D., H.D.'s mother, and baby Perdita.

Sir John gave McAlmon funding for Contact Press, that published some of the bright lights of modernism—among them, James Joyce, Gertrude Stein, Djuna Barnes, H.D., Bryher, and Mina Loy. As Bryher's husband, McAlmon provided a cloak of marital respectability for her and H.D. One of his favorite haunts was Paris, where Bryher and H.D. were to meet Gertrude Stein and Alice B. Toklas. Bryher also met and became fast friends with Adrienne Monnier, the proprietor of the bookshop, La Maison des Amis des Livres, and her lover, Sylvia Beach, who with her help, established Shakespeare and Co., the iconic English language bookstore that was to become the nexus for poets, artists, and playwrights in Paris during that time and for decades after. Bryher's mother sent a plaster bust of Shakespeare as mascot for the store—the "post-office" used by Bryher and McAlmon to correlate their stories of togetherness, while living distinct lives.

But McAlmon's decadence proved too much for Bryher. She divorced him, marrying filmmaker and photographer, Kenneth Mcpherson, and adopted Perdita (aka "Pup') in 1927. Kenneth was not only a lover of H.D., but a creative force in his own right and a good friend to both women; theirs was an unconventional family. He and Bryher built Kenwin in the Bauhaus style, in Switzerland, its name deriving from the first syllables of their names—Kenneth and Winifred. Kenneth also directed three experimental films, the most complete, *Borderline* (1930), featuring Paul Robeson, his wife, Eslanda, H.D. and Bryher. With an avant-garde montage, it exposed undercurrents of white supremacy.

In 1933, Bryher witnessed brown shirts and military operations in Berlin, and wrote a piece openly criticizing Britain in the shutdown of *Close Up*, the trio's experimental film magazine, "What Will You Do In the War?"[9] She warned of heightened militarism, displaced persons with meagre luggage. At age fourteen, Perdita marched in Hyde Park to protest Nazism, and she felt her whole youth a build-up to war.

H.D. and Bryher's relationship was complex, involving them in numerous "psychic" triangles, including one with Freud, with whom Bryher arranged for H.D. to consult in 1933 and 1934, during the poet's writer's block. While H.D. was in analysis, Bryher widely distributed *J'Accuse!*, the pamphlet by S.M. Salomon, published by the World Alliance for Combating Anti-Semitism, that contained numerous evidentiary photographs and testimonials, gathered from reputable news agencies and eye-witnesses, exposing the barbarity against Jews: torture, beatings, interrogation, normalized through hate articles and armed militia.[10] H.D. asked Bryher for some for Freud and others. H.D. told her that Freud "broke his great analytical rule of not noticing mags" in picking up *J'ACCUSE*; he "almost wept" that the English had done this.[11] Still H.D. resisted what she saw as Bryher's "warpath" mentality, wanting to savor her hours with the aged Freud. Impressed with Bryher, Freud called her a "northern explorer," though asking if she was Jewish, he answered the naive question that there "was no trace." A skeptical Bryher: "So I said rubbish I wanted to be a Jew because David was tiny but slew Goliath."[12] Freud saw her savior complex writ large. At this point, Bryher embarked on a six-year crusade of rescuing refugees from the Nazis, obtaining visas, and even buying passports on the black market.

In 1936, Bryher warned in her new publication, *Life & Letters*: "Every time that you laugh about not having the time nor the brains to bother about foreign affairs, you will just go and water the lupins, you are making it a little more certain that you will lose eventually, your garden, your home, and your life."[13] Bryher echoes this in the words of one of her characters in Beowulf: "How does being an ostrich save one from disaster?"

————

When Hitler invaded Poland, our couple was at Kenwin in Switzerland with the psychoanalysts, Melitta and Walter Schmideberg (Melitta was the daughter of the eminent child psychologist, Melanie Klein), huddling around the wireless. Two days later, Britain, France, Australia and New Zealand declared war. Bryher imagined herself during the Great War "struggling up the lane in the Isle of Wight towards the post office as if the intervening years had been wiped out with some dark sponge."[14] A soldier in World War I, Walter spoke of its first dead. H.D. wrote George Plank that "the last 20 [years] have simply dropped out, simply gone and one is just there back in ones [sic] early middle age."[15] She coaxed herself: "I must pull myself together and live or die. I don't think I'll do the latter."[16]

With war announced, another abyss opened: Bryher's mother, Lady Hannah Ellerman, died on September 17, 1939 in Cornwall. Bryher could not make it back in time to be by her mother's bed-side. That same month Freud died. Relieved Lady Ellerman and Freud would be spared this new war, the couple nonetheless felt a terrible sense of loss and time disjunction. Both bi-centurians—with Bryher born in Queen

Victoria's reign, like the teashop owners in the novel, held a panoramic sense of seismic change. H.D. and Bryher were middle-aged—53 and 45, respectively, when WWII began. While H.D. strove to survive through "ancient rubrics" and "spiritual realism" in the first section of *Trilogy*, *Walls Do Not Fall*, published by Oxford in 1944 (though written almost simultaneously to *Beowulf*), Bryher could only live moment to moment, feeling "war was Time in all its ponderous duration. [...] People must live, but sometimes waiting in line, she wondered why."

———

The so-called "phony war" lasted from approximately September 1939 until July 1940, with the Germans embroiled elsewhere on the continent. Many in the populace, such as Robert Herring, editor of *Life & Letters*, felt "in the dark" on many points. Advising that "[g]asmasks are practically second-nature," along with hat and gloves, Herring prepared the returnees, not knowing Bryher would stay behind.[17] The sidewalk edges were chalked white to prevent falls during a raid. Air-wardens commandeered the streets. In *Beowulf*, Bryher describes how people sometimes had to crawl to shelters.

H.D. took the last Orient Express back to London in November 1939. At 48 Lowndes Square, the flat H.D. inhabited after her Freud sessions in 1934, H.D. saw London brace for attack with the mandatory blackouts, fire watchers, stretcher vans, shelters, and mobile canteens. She perceived how gender standards had altered, conveying to Bryher that "the streets are full of attractive girls in long blue trousers, ambulance, and other oddments in short skirts and short hair [...] the ambulance drivers use their blue pants, like yours and Pup's. All very familiar and sea-shorish."[18] Both H.D. and Perdita noted the subtle but eerie switch from white bulbs to blue. London was pulling itself together.

H.D. lunched with Perdita regularly at "The Warming Pan" where she went for "escapes" to find a shadow of the familiar "old world" of London. Adversity initially fed H.D.'s magic. Seeing herself as "analyst poet," with a small fund Bryher had set up, she reached out to help others in extremes whom she met at the tearoom, or those who, like herself, had survived World War I. H.D. wrote her friend Silvia Dobson, "I am expecting Br., end Nov or early Dec. But I am here, hale and hearty, moving about like a fire-fly. I find the black-out very beautiful and exciting, too," remarking upon an air-warden who "found a chink of light."[19] Perdita recognized "Kat," (H.D.'s nickname) as a species distinct from her other mother, "Fido" (Bryher's nickname), diagnosing: "She has one of those poetic, detached natures which see the best in all, even the black-out; she finds it so beautiful, the emergency lamps are like fairy candles, girls in tin helmets like at a fancy dress party."[20] Perdita admitted she herself couldn't stop swearing. She knew the blackout wasn't likely to revitalize Bryher, though H.D. compared her to "a little Atlas." Bryher confirmed to Norman Holmes Pearson (1909–1975), a professor of English poetry at Yale, who would remain close friends of both women into the future: "H.D. seems to find black outs poetical, I am sure I shall find it depressing."[21]

Bryher's grief-laden mind (for her mother, for the past) was clouded. Although she came to Lowndes Square in December, she left again for Kenwin in January 1940, compelled to return to help her housekeeper and friend Elsie Volkart move to a small house in Pully (with Bryher's beloved Claudi and pups). She also needed to burn evidence of her refugee work, having aided endangered Jewish students, analysts, and others persecuted by the Nazis. Perdita's former governess, the Austrian Alice Modern and her husband Franz Alt, whom Bryher had urged to apply for exit visas early and supplied them with $5,000 to establish themselves, were now safe in New York.[22] Alice's sister, Klara Modern, in London with funds from Bryher for analysis, vowed to fight for her adopted country and pledged to be interned, if it would in any way help the British.

Throughout February and March, H.D. reported "general war demoralization."[23] Braving it on her own, she felt an unexpected euphoria: "4:30 black-out and then get up in the morning to fog. But I have many chats with people in shops and everywhere. We in the city are very much at one."[24]

Almost with no opposition, Hitler's blitzkrieg conquered Europe at an alarming rate in the first months of the year: Poland, Czechoslovakia, Hungary, and Yugoslavia. Bryher told H.D. she didn't know exactly when she could return to London, planning to arrive by April, but German military advances made this tricky.

Not a second too soon, Churchill took over as Prime Minister on May 7, 1940. Fight, and fight on they must, he boomed on radio broadcasts, convincing the public through his impish yet stern rhetoric to toughing the disaster head-on, though they were grievously unprepared. A month after Norway's capitulation, the Germans invaded Holland and Belgium. The British Expeditionary Force and French troops could not stand up to the "Blitzkrieg," rupturing defense lines to seize airfields. The Luftwaffe made it impossible to re-supply. French regiments crumbled; with the Germans moving into the low countries, the majority of Allied Troops corralled at Dunkirk.

During the critical days from May 26, to June 4, 1940, Churchill offered the British public a stake in their own survival, commanding all boats, whether civilian or military, of any demonstrable size to evacuate Dunkirk. His B.B.C. plea received a thunderous response. H.D. exulted in what seemed "almost a religious spectacle": The battle of the ports was something out of all time, wonderful. The merchant marine came in for a lot of glory. Tugs were all taken off the Thames, all fire-boats, trawlers, fishing smacks, lifeboats and so on, took that terrible trip over and over."[25] This coordinated effort cheered H.D.; this Bryher missed.

Fretting about Perdita, H.D. knew it was a "hang-over" from the last war: "This is truly for all, a spiritual rebirth. If ones bodies [sic] stand it."[26] On their anniversary, H.D. told Bryher London might be "more to your vibration when you return."[27] Though stationed in the country, Edith Sitwell expressed: "The last fortnight has been on such a gigantic scale, that everything in history since the Crucifixion seems dwarfed—only Shakespeare could do justice to it."[28] H.D. had her heroes in the R.A.F., led by Air Marshall, Hugh Dowding. Still British propriety crashed; people wandered about with coats over pajamas; women stopped wearing stockings. H.D. noticed the new generation's short skirts and cut several of Bryher's dresses in half, so they'd fit her, but it felt like "castrating" Bryher![29]

On June 9, Sylvia Beach urged Bryher to come to France immediately, offering Adrienne's cellar. The German tanks, however, outflanked the Maginot Line. While gunned down and bombed on June 14, civilians fled Paris *en masse*. By June 22, 1940, France signed an armistice with Germany, leaving a small unoccupied zone. After France surrendered, readiness was all. Magnetized by the living drama, at the tea-shop and Lowndes, H.D. felt it her duty was to be "in readiness, as for anyone of the crowd who may need psychic sustenance," telling Bryher: "I consider that it is necessary to hold this place as for you, first and foremost, a little fortress. It is always ready. That is my chief raison-d'etre. Then Pup (Perdita)."[30] With exuberance over Dunkirk fading, H.D. craved Bryher's presence: "You said early June, then mid-June, then just June!"[31]

From June through September 1940, the couple, who both compulsively corresponded, could not write full letters, only "keeping the wire open," as H.D. put it. Marianne Moore forwarded letters between them, for fear of the censor. H.D. suffered "homesickness." England felt temporarily "gone." After all, she was psychically linked to South Audley Street, the late Lady Ellerman, and Bryher. H.D. sent Bryher birthday wishes on September 2, shopping between air-raid sirens. In honor of Bryher, she "now recognizes the big gun, our special Big Ben and feel very comforted when it booms off," admitting "I never thought I would have a personal feeling about a gun, before."[32] Having endured "three weeks of constant hammering," she acclimated to a "nine o'clock symphony." "Every morning," H.D. wrote Moore, "is a sort of special gift; a new day to be cherished and loved, a DAY that seems to love back in return."[33] Proximity to death incited H.D towards its apparent grand opponent: love. Glad Moore and her mother were "spared," she bragged she was "sorry, too, as our fervour and intensity gives new life to the very bones." Urged to return to the States, H.D. resisted.

"Fido," however felt trapped, while Swiss officials told her to make haste. A man, whose son she had given a book from Sylvia's Beach bookshop in Paris, arranged her transport. It was a grueling, dangerous journey through Barcelona and Lisbon, partly on a cramped coach, another leg on a bus riddled with bullet holes Bryher suspected were from the Spanish Civil War, only to await plane transport. Anxiously moving through checkpoints, she travelled with a young Jewish woman, Grace Irwin, daughter of one of her mother's friends. She saw men green with hunger; other horrors she kept for *Beowulf*, such as the hands of a man "broken by rifle butts" whom the Nazis had left for dead.

Touching down at Poole in England during an air raid, Bryher dwelled on the ludicrous nature of her trip to London: "got here from Switzerland. How? Oh, only by a German plane with an Italian pilot. [...] Officially Spanish" to land in "the middle of the Blitz." Forced to stop several times due to rail damage, Bryher finally arrived at Lowndes Square on September 28. H.D. had, in fact, just ducked out for lunch at the "Warming Pan." Bryher sat on the steps, reeling, surveying the blacked-out windows and general ruin. With no illusion the war would be over by Christmas, she felt "forced back into the cage and misery of the first war."[34]

———

When H.D. spotted Bryher sitting on her steps on her suitcase, she held her hand out, guided Bryher towards the sand piles, showing her how to put out incendiaries. Perdita was staying on what she called an officers' camp-bed in Bryher's room. Like one sleepwalker to another, H.D. initiated Bryher into war-ways. The sirens started up; they climbed down to the lower floor. Upon waking, Bryher confronted the "war made new," exploiting earth's skies and seas. Herring wrote: "So you made it," followed with, "It certainly is a fabulous time at which to drop in. Congratulations."[35]

Thinking nothing would faze her after her journey, Bryher's first reaction was terrible shock, summed up in her anecdote about a woman who ran an eel shop who left only briefly, and returned to find it gone. Such immediate vanishings gave Bryher a sense of unreality, akin to what she felt among the ruins of the Parthenon with H.D. on their travels in 1920. Only now the ruins were in ongoing process. She used Pearson as safety valve, "[t]he blackout cuts out half one's life. Travel about England is intensely uncomfortable and difficult,"[36] further retailing for their growing bond: "ignorance of what is going on in Europe makes one howl with rage. The French for instance loathe Pétain [...] and the officials here want to believe he is a noble elderly soldier." Spain felt "merely a German province," where she recounted hearing only German spoken. Bryher uniquely cultivated a bird's eye-view. "Believe me," she wrote, "there is nothing romantic about bombardments, gunfire, black out, food rations, and the awful claustrophobia of being stuck on an island. My slogan is that I am perfectly willing to die for England but absolutely hostile to being asked to live on the island."[37] Bryher described her and H.D. cooking supper by a single candle, training themselves not to swallow if the anti-aircraft guns were firing.

Keeping up American contacts, Bryher wrote H.D.'s friend, Mary Herr, that London was a "mouse-trap," and that she had arrived in the middle of the Blitz, watching "the tiny houses go down like toys."[38] These details fed her writing in *Beowulf*, begun in October, written during the day on a "broad window ledge," and she told how once a warden came by at night, thinking her typing on her bed was some kind of signaling.[39] She recorded the hollowness in watching solid structures dematerialize: "The heaviest buildings had a fragile air as if children had cut them out of coloured paper and stuck them up in school with cardboard supports. If you poked a brick you were surprised that it did not crumple like a balloon." Bryher found adjustment difficult: "Life here can only be called peculiar. It goes on perfect normally with gigantic gaps."[40] She vented: "I knew it was coming and nobody would listen to me when I told them about the German preparations and I watched helplessly while we gave the Germans every advantage possible and slid into this state of utter muddle ourselves."

Beowulf allowed Bryher to dramatize the visceral, noting in her narrative descriptions, "a new smell for London," not like "plague pits," but "the smell of wet dust and burnt brick," and she observed a road "ankle deep in glass," with "broad jagged splinters and heaps of brittle crumbs." Language strained to approximate visions of craters pocking the streets; the sizzling desertion, with those who joined the "great migration to the country," as she calls it.

By the end of 1940 in London, many were forced to "live" in shelters. Bryher was shocked, writing Moore that it was "unbelievable what the people are enduring"; she described the scene in detail: "most of them sleeping on the ground in excessively damp shelters or sitting up on chairs under the staircase or parked in the tubes. It is really more than any book ever could describe."[41] Marianne Moore empathized with her friend: "the unnatural danger of the blackout; and the obstacles to getting a job. When one is panting with desire to help the country win, and what is more rare—equipped at every point as you are, to do it—I know the white hot intensity of some of your wartime reflections." Moore provided salve for Bryher's "hide," knowing her desire to heal, to give and to act: "But there is a certain consolation, don't you think, in the sense that each of us is scourged with the very same sense of frustration—an illusion after all, Bryher. What we feel is the sinews of war." Within the temporal confusion, Bryher saw young girls, like Eve in the novel, tramping down the stairs of the tearoom's lodging; one also sees a bit of Bryher in her Colonel Ferguson, seeking a government position, rebuffed because he had been in Switzerland after India, his age counting against him.

Bryher gunned for the Establishment, which she separated from Churchill, who she thought received paltry gratitude for rescuing London, the world even, when he was put out of office by Labor in 1946. Matter of fact about losing their *Life & Letters* Maiden Lane office, Bryher wrote Pearson: "[it] went, a time bomb so no casualties and we saved everything but had to clear out as ceilings fell on desks." Bryher hoarded a tonnage of paper before war started to be sure she could keep her journal afloat. Another of *Beowulf*'s cast, Adelaide Spenser, in London with a military husband, bought "sixty pounds of marmalade," for barter for eggs after the Munich Conference in 1938. Bryher deliberately put herself near everyday Londoners, surveying the wreckage of glass, dirt, damp and even flesh. The Germans took up where they left off, with vicious attacks between December 27 and New Year's Eve. Churchill posted extra fire watchers around St. Paul's Cathedral to extinguish incendiaries, but as Bryher's novel observes, there were limited resources for "the middle groups" who "suffer most in war and the Victorian doctrine that hard work is its own reward flops at once in a time of national disaster."

Still holding a visa for America, Bryher expressed to Pearson: "What is it like. The house rocks like the *Normandie* in a gale, all the things happen that you see on a movie, and hear [...] Shells whistling, guns thundering, explosions, one thinks nothing can survive the night and crawls up from the basement to listen to the early news and dear B.B.C says 'last night's attacks were on a somewhat smaller scale than usual.' Then one rushes out to listen to what the milkman, the taxi driver, the porter and the shopgirl have to say about the B.B.C."[42] This sentiment found its way into Beowulf as the heiress joined London citizens, and in fact her Angelina, the teashop proprietor most like Bryher, with her political meetings and what H.D. liked to call Bryher's "enthusiasms," who probably spent time, like Angelina, "mimick[ing] the announcer: 'there was slight enemy activity over London in the early hours of last evening.'" When Bryher went to obtain her identity card and ration book she was stopped by the porter, once an acrobat in Switzerland, who knew her lake "upside-down."[43] Startled, she wrote Annie Reich, a psychoanalyst she helped emigrate to New York, about this phenomenon: "I chat incorrigibly to people in the street and am acquiring a mass of miscellaneous knowledge, one friend of mine is over sixty and suddenly decided that she had to make munitions."[44] Bryher was herself vitalized by war through such encounters, and her devotion to H.D.

She mourned in her chronicle, "the absurdity of it all, dropping of balls upon the ninepin houses." This felt vulnerability she expressed by "going out" and facing it; H.D. stayed close within her walls, incanting prayers for those in danger, and for her own psychic survival, culminating in *The Walls Do Not Fall*, dedicated to Bryher for their previous travel to Egypt in 1920 and now London; H.D. telescoped these geographies, seeing the fragile houses instead as roofless shrines, "ruin everywhere, yet as the fallen roof / leaves the sealed room,"[45] she sought to conjure "protection for the scribe"[46] through her very writing. H.D.'s recognition that their shelter was imperiled drove Bryher's sense in *Beowulf* of "walls being alive." She transported Horatio Rasleigh (she gave her real life contacts fictional names in the novel), born in approximately 1872, subsisting on an aunt's monthly pittance, into her novel, as living above the "Warming Pan"; though never meeting this man, because of his quaint paintings of ships, she corresponded with him for years, sending him stipends.[47] In Beowulf, he winces at the "wretched" noises on the radio, anxious about his loss of patrons of his hand-painted greeting cards.

Pledging no raid would scare her after what she endured in her harrowing trip back to London, Bryher put on her beaten leather jacket, market gloves, braved the queues, turned in registration forms, and prowled the ruins, grieving the loss of her father's long-gone world. As chronicler and griever, she almost immediately came upon the genesis of her working title for *Beowulf*:

> The raids were heavy throughout October. I went
> out gloomily one morning with my basket to get

our rations and saw a huge crater at the end of Basil Street. Somebody had fetched a large plaster bulldog, I assume from Harrods because they were then on sale there, and stuck it on guard beside the biggest pile of rubble.[48]

"Comrade Bulldog" was "conceived" in a flash. Her Angelina was not "a symbol of gallantry but of common sense," while Selina, perhaps speaking for H.D., questioned the sense of carrying a plaster bulldog and setting it in the hearth of a tearoom. Selina found it vulgar—as much as Angelina protests: "'Beowulf is a symbol of us, colleague," for "'comrade simply didn't suit'" the dignified Selina.

H.D. was well aware that Bryher took to the "outer" world better than she did, describing Bryher's humanist forays: "a wonder with her good deeds and constant care; she knows all the people in the neighborhood and when I go out with her, it is positively embarrassing as her progress is one triumphal procession. Someone's teeth here, someone's gout there, someone's baby there, someone's son in the near-east somewhere else—" and finally, speaking for them both, she looked "forward to [him] joining [their] village life."[49] After Norman Pearson came to London in 1943 to supervise spy-craft, he hired Perdita for the U.S. Office of Strategic Services (OSS), a precursor to the Central Intelligence Agency. Though Pearson arranged a job in Washington for her, Bryher desired proximity to H.D. and Perdita.

———

The novel *Beowulf* opens on the last day of Horatio Rashleigh, born in the Victorian age. Modernist in its form of twelve chapters, it is "a day and night in the life" of the Blitz, it provides key-hole glimpses, set forth in plain if spunky language, knowing "there were no words" to describe the predicament of Londoners during the Blitz. The saving grace is the tea shop, "a cross between a village shop and family doctor": "You walked up to the 'Warming Pan' if you wanted a recipe for quince marmalade or if Auntie had trapped a swarm of bees in her garden and had written for advice."

Bryher's "Warming Pan" is a nexus, where a number of lives meet: along with Selina and Angelina, the retired Colonel roaring to get back into action; a woman waiting to see a friend coming in from the country; Horatio, the older rheumatic gentleman; the young working girl, Eva, who plays jazz, sports bobbed hair and rushes out, "like a fledgling man-at-arms," encapsulating the new generation's "freedoms." Written in the style of free indirect discourse, the narrative flits from mind to mind. Bryher knit everyday Londoners who were not always able to "keep calm and carry on" (as the posters instructed) during horrific threats and massive changes.

Angelina and Selina bear shadow resemblances to Bryher and H.D. themselves. The former semi-mocks herself through Angelina, who a quarter in, emerges in a slow cinematic unveiling: "At first only scarlet gloves and the tip of a beret were visible," before she sets down a plaster dog, "almost life size, with a piratical scowl painted on his black muzzle." The impractical plaster dog is the heart of the novel. With her imagist sensibility (learned from H.D.)—the practice of condensing in one image a number of related ideas or motifs—the artificial canine becomes provisional, a shadow of the emblematic British Empire, and thus more endearing.

Angelina boldly carries the "vulgar" icon into the eighteenth-century tearoom.

Bryher channeled through Angelina's point of view, explaining that she found it opposite the "Food Office": "'I can't keep a dog, I know, in the raids, but it's so cheerless without one. I was afraid at first you might be tempted to call him Winnie, but then I thought, no, here is an emblem of the whole of us, so gentle, so determined ...'" Of course we hear Winifred in Winnie (Bryher's original middle birth name). The nickname "Fido" represented Bryher's fidelity to H.D., her fiduciary know-how, and her tenacity when taking up the cudgels for underdogs.

The actual teashop Bryher and H.D. regularly patronized was put out of business by a raid in 1941, making the book elegiac.[50] Bryher's novel maintains an essentially Enlightenment vision that coffeehouses and tearooms are public spaces that exist for exchange of thought. Her Selina reasons that the times wanted "a new and quite other vocabulary" to comprehend what was beyond human comprehension. Her tea shop, Selina believed, helped "morale": "For if clients came into lunch and went off cheerfully afterwards, they, in turn, would affect their relatives and their maids." Bryher found Selina inspiring, "especially on such a cold, dreary morning, to think how much one solitary woman could do in defence of her native land." "Tearooms had a special meaning for Selina." They were "the perfect meeting place." Bryher later memorialized, "Selina was a symbol to me of the essential soul of England," in her desire to maintain quality, noting the couple's difficulty during the war because "most of their customers had gone into the country or joined the Women's Services."[51]

Bryher held that the British government, in failing to listen to Churchill, had cheated the public of a proper wartime diet. Never one to indulge herself, she wondered where her country's sirloins, cheddars and beer had gone. She knew H.D., already lacking in protein, had trouble eating when harassed. England could have imported better food, but it "had flung away much of the nation's foreign reserves in panic selling after the Fall of France."[52] There was too much "austerity and restraint."[53] An obsession with food supply revealed her provider-complex.

Part of the minimal plot, the drama of her tea shop proprietors was that they only used farm eggs, but now only rationed egg powder was allotted for such shops as theirs; but since they hadn't signed on initially, they fretted about necessary forms, or not being able to bake at all. As unimportant as a tearoom might seem, Bryher unveiled Selina's invisible life-and-death struggle to survive, while helping make wartime life a bit more nutritious and solacing.

While the teashop is a locus of community, it bears the marks of the war. The posted notice, 'Careless Talk Costs Lives,' part of a propaganda campaign, reminded her "of a morning in the last war when she had stood in line for hours to get new ration books." Selina herself didn't like the sign, feeling "[l]ife ought to be generous, she felt, wildly generous." The link between rationing and espionage posters reminded that liberty is sometimes as hard to obtain as butter in wartime.

Bryher, as Angelina, compared the raids "to a film, but the screen was at least concrete" compared to "this concentrated bombing." It simply narrowed life to survival, without cohesion. "'So this is the twentieth century,'" her Selina "snorted." This declaration occurs before Bryher delivers a final quiet slow-motion chapter with herself as witness, with the painful sense of shared precarity. We sense her "procession" with H.D. among Londoners, but here she takes us to the visceral core of war response.

After many descents to the shelter, Selina never knew climbing the short set of stairs could be so exhausting. The siren goes off, and dutifully, Selina climbs up to rouse the elderly Horatio, who resists her efforts. Her neck, "permanently stiff," she lugged blankets and necessities down the dark stairs and through the hall to the dark street, where she almost drops her burden, hearing explosions beginning: "Half the sky seemed to explode over their heads and crash." When they arrive at the shelter, knitting needles resume between crashes and explosions: it was "as if they were lying on the bottom of the well with nothing overhead." (H.D.'s "shrine open to the sky" of *Walls* echoes.) Suddenly, "the walls lifted with a roar at that moment and split, and rushed towards each other in a cascade of noise, plaster, and crumbling bricks." Selina discovers, looking through thick smoke, the staircase Eve traversed was no more. Angelina reassures—"remember, partner, here we are alive," excited that Beowulf survived the raid as well. "Humor is protection," she declared, plotting to strap a basket on Beowulf, set him on wheels, and serve their wares. They'd need a hawker's license. Its mutely horrific end was appropriate—for after all, such events happened every day and night in London and elsewhere. The last line bandies a mock stiff-upper-lip response: "It is embarrassing to be caught in a raid."

———

Bryher expected the British would suppress the publication of *Beowulf* because it too closely recorded actual Blitz conditions, believing the public wanted to forget the war—and would dismiss her so-called "little people"—the shopkeepers and their customers—trying to make life a bit gayer. Adrienne Monnier called it a "petit classique;" the book's brevity at 201 pages calls attention to Bryher's goal: she wanted to give the everyday citizen]a reflection of their struggle. It was first published in French, through Monnier's own press, Mercure de France, on April 18, 1946, but the translator, Helene Malvant, was unsure of the title. Sylvia Beach said "[i]f the French have never heard of Beowulf they are going to do so now."[54] Both Sylvia and Adrienne were sworn "Beowulfians." They recognized themselves as the two teashop owners, Selina and Angelina (the couples even had identical initials). In a sense, Bryher wrote the book in homage to female couples, as herself and H.D., whose relationships were obscured by still governing Victorian rules, and blindness to variations in sexual identity and desire.

After finishing the work in 1944, Bryher put it aside to write her first historical novel, *The Fourteenth of October*, portraying the Norman Conquest. She told Pearson she viewed those invaders as the "Nazis of their day." He introduced Bryher to Kurt Wolff, who, along with his wife Helen, had an imprint at Pantheon Books in New York. Wolff published Bryher's novels, including the *Fourteenth of October* (1952), *The Player's Boy* (1953) *The Roman Wall* (1954), and finally, *Beowulf* (1956). Its publication was advertised in a quarter-page of *The New York Times*, alongside H.D.'s *Tribute to Freud*, published the same year but like *Beowulf*, finished more than a decade earlier, in 1944. "Together, at last," wrote H.D., happy to see

Beowulf and her own memoir of Freud out at the same time. H.D.'s lyricism joined Bryher's documentarian point of view, both fueled by great humor, and humility.

The American edition of *Beowulf* bears the dedication, both an epistle and an epitaph:

TO

Sylvia Beach

AND THE MEMORY OF

Adrienne Monnier

The dedication is significant. After all, the "Warming Pan" offered sustenance when there was none. In some ways, it operated similarly to Beach's Shakespeare & Co. or Adrienne's shop as not just sites for commerce, but also for cultivating creativity in a dark time. Bryher held faith with her early *Beowulf* supporter, Adrienne, diagnosed in 1954 with "la maladie Ménière," with spells of terrible vertigo, dizziness, vomiting, and whistling in the ears, making her life unlivable.[55] With no cure, Adrienne's sister and Sylvia assisted her suicide by giving her a lethal dose of pills on June 19, 1955. Bryher memorialized this act: "When the time came she showed us how to die and hardly a day passes now when I do not miss her."[56] H.D. heard this news from Bryher by phone, and wrote immediately to Sylvia to "accept my heart's devotion-a double devotion": she couldn't imagine them apart.[57] Bryher posed with Sylvia Beach, with the photo of H.D. by Man Ray between them: the date of the photo is uncertain but was post-WWII, reflecting as biographer Virginia Smyers puts it, "she never lost faith in H.D.'s art."[58]

———

33

A handful of favorable reviews came out when Pantheon published the English version of *Beowulf,* and in the "Briefly Noted" section of *The New Yorker* the reviewer exclaimed that Bryher, "that very gifted, very human writer, tells a small, resounding story."[59] "Small" again, but a dynamo. Marianne Moore commended Bryher's deft combination of prosaic and heroic.[60] She spoke with choral helplessness through her characters. As she put it in her book, there would always exist a chasm between those bombed upon and those not, yet it seemed New York was ready to start looking at what films *had not* showed. Robert Parris's appreciative review of it as "emotional," compared *Beowulf* favorably to *The Fair Game* by Constantine Fitzgibbons', both "about people living among live bombs and dying friends," but more notably aligned hers with the macabre realism of Henry Green. By 1956, when these reviews were written, Bryher had come into her own, described by Parris in his review as "a lady who had the courage to return to England from Switzerland at the outbreak of war, and who obviously knows what bad tea, margarine, cakes made with egg powder and sleeping in public shelters mean to an Englishman." Recognizing in Bryher's steady absurd portrait of the "idea of morale is to carry on as if nothing at all unusual were happening," John Hutchens praised her "quiet, affecting, formal understated report."[61]

———

Beowulf's stark humor makes it a faithful companion when times are uncertain. The fact that it appeared in French first highlights its circuitous route to publication: a novel of London, only publishable in Paris or New York. In republishing the work, the hope is that those in the twenty-first century will find their own "plaster" reflection in *Beowulf*, learning history's jolting repetitions—as well as finding in Bryher an insightful chronicler, observing the quotidian details of life in their most unreal and extreme circumstances. She had learned from the philosopher Walter Benjamin that any triumphal conquest depended on devastation and plunder, with the victors recording history. In *Beowulf*, she mourned lost devotions, fantasizing being among "anonymous craftsmen who spent a lifetime on some obscure corner of a cathedral wall."

Both Bryher and H.D. wrote some of their best work during the Second World War with an eye to writing as survival and resistance. Bryher took on the external world, complemented by H.D.'s more inner one. They sought to find through historical time-travel precedents for war—and peace, and if in fact, they were heading as H.D. believed, into a supposed "Aquarian age." They were the generation that saw the quick erosion of Victorian life, though its repressiveness lingered. The constant disruption made it possible, according to H.D., for Bryher to write in episodes. By the 1950s, H.D. looked back nostalgically on Bryher reading parts aloud as they emerged while she and Perdita stitched.

Bryher perceived herself among exiles "scattered across Europe as deputy ambassadors, carrying ideas or even goods to people who would never come in contact," a premise with the "emissaries" of "secret wisdom," and "living remnant" that *Walls* conveyed in a more literary register.[62] *Trilogy* believed in talismans, charms, amulets; Bryher's mascot bulldog was a bitter-sweet charm. On a brighter note, Bryher recorded in her journal that she finished *Beowulf* on January 18, 1944, but she knew the English would have none of it. H.D. had good news for Pearson: Oxford wanted to publish an American copy of "W A L L S."[63] With this in mind, the more raw world of *Beowulf* would make a clarifying teaching companion to *Trilogy,* especially *The Walls Do Not Fall,* that witnesses "*dust and powder fill our lungs / our bodies blunder*" as well as **its** faith without faith, a search: "*we are voyagers, discoverers / of the not-known, / / the unrecorded: we have no map.*" A productive dialogue between these texts, both written at Lowndes Square, widens the lens so we see each woman's struggle as "shock knit with terror," recording the precursors to our own contemporary sense of omnipresent war, a digital blitz of sorts, and a geopolitical communal helplessness —and, yet, hope.

ENDNOTES

1   The University of Wisconsin collected Development and *Two
    Selves* in a single volume in 2000; Paris Press has published
    several of her novels (*Visa for Avalon: A Novel* [2004] and
    The Player's Boy [2006]) along with her influential memoir,
    The Heart to Artemis: A Writer's Memoirs (2006).

2   *The Days of Mars: A Memoir,* 1940–1946 (New York:
    Harcourt Brace, 1971), 12.

3   *Paris 1900*, translated into French like *Beowulf,* was first
    published by Adrienne Monnier in 1936.

4   *Heart to Artemis*, 16–17.

5   Bryher to H.D., March 20, 1919. All letters unless otherwise
    noted are from the Beinecke Rare Book and Manuscript
    Library, Yale University.

6   *HA*, 110–111.

7   *Ibid*, 115–116.

8   H.D. to Bryher, November 29, 1934.

9   *Close Up* 10.2 (June 1933): 188.

10 *J'Accuse*, Salomon House, 33 St. Jame's Street, London, S.W. 1: 6.

11 H.D. to Bryher, May 16, 1933.

12 Bryher to Macpherson, March 31, 1933.

13 "*The Crisis: September*', *Life and Letters To-Day*, 19/25 (Nov. 1938): 1.

14 Bryher, *Heart to Artemis*, 288.

15 H.D to George Plank, September 25, 1939.

16 Ibid.

17 Herring to Bryher September 21, 1939.

18 H.D. to Bryher, November 11, 1939.

19 H.D. to Silvia Dobson, November 16, 1939.

20 Perdita to Bryher, November 14, 1939.

21 Bryher to Pearson, December 2, 1939.

22 Conversation with James Alt, July 2018; as a son of Alice Modern, he learned of Bryher's generosity, and claimed she saved his whole family.

23 H.D. to Bryher, March 5, 1940.

24 Ibid., November 11, 1939.

25 Ibid, June 5, 1940.

26 Ibid. June 7, 1940.

27 Ibid. July 17, 1940.

28 Edith Sitwell to Pavel Tchelitchew; June 6, 1940. Quoted in Greene's *Edith Sitwell: Avant Garde Poet, English Genius* (New York: Virago Press, 2011), 284.

29 H.D. to Bryher, May 1, 1940.

30 Ibid, May 31, 1940.

31 Ibid., May 30, 1940.

32 Ibid, September 2, 1940.

33 H.D. to Moore, September 24, 1940.

34 *Heart to Artemis*, 307.

35 Herring to Bryher, September 30, 1940.

36 Bryher to Pearson, December 5, 1940.

37 Ibid, January 1941.

38 Bryher to Mary Herr, October 17, 1940. Bryn Mawr Bryher Papers.

39 *Days of Mars*, 14.

40 Bryher to Pearson, January 19, 1941.

41 Moore to Bryher, October 14, 1940; Rosenbach Museum and Library.

42 Bryher to Pearson, December 5, 1940.

43 Bryher, *Days of Mars*, 8.

44 Bryher to Annie Reich, January 5, 1941.

45 *Walls Do Not Fall* in *Trilogy* New York: New Directions 1973: 3.

46 H.D. to Pearson, [nd] 1943; cited in *Between Poetry and History: The Letters of H.D. and Norman Holmes Pearson*, edited by Donna Krolik Hollenberg (Iowa City: University of Iowa Press, 997), 30–33.

47 *Days of Mars*, 15.

48 *Ibid.*, 12-13.

49 H.D. to Pearson, May 2, 1943; *Between History and Poetry*, 22.

50 Annette Debo in *Within the Walls* notes that H.D. requested bequests from Bryher for the two women, Miss Docker and Miss Venables, after they lost their business. Gainesville: University Press of Florida, 2014: 49. Debo's collection of H.D.'s uncollected stories and poems from the Blitz is accompanied by her deft research into the period. This book could **fruitfully join** for a class on H.D. and Bryher during World War II.

51 *Days of Mars*, 12.

52 *Ibid*, 5.

53 Ibid., 5.

54 Beach to Bryher, January 28, 1948.

55 Sylvia to Bryher, October 25, 1954.

56 *HA*, 209.

57 H.D. to Sylvia Beach, June 22, 1955.

58 Gillian Hanscombe & Virgina L. Smyers, *Writing for their Lives: The Modernist Women 1910–1940*. (London: The Women's Press, 1987), 46.

59 *New Yorker*, September 1, 1956.

60 *New York Post*, August 26, 1956.

61 *Chicago Tribute*, August 27, 1956.

62 Bryher, *Days of Mars*, 76.

63 H.D. to Pearson, February 24, 1944. Hollenberg, *Between History and Poetry*, 34. WDNF was published in 1944, *Tribute to the Angels* in 1945, and *Flowering of the Rod* in 1946, published successively by Oxford University Press: it became *Trilogy*.

BEOWULF

1

THOSE WRETCHED people had turned on the radio again. Horatio shifted the bedclothes with great caution and felt for the switch. Formerly he had flung his curtains wide last thing in the evening, but in this miserable blackout he could see nothing without a light. Seven o'clock. There was no need, absolutely no need, to consider rising for at least two hours. First of all his doctor, his very kind doctor, had bidden him stay in bed, "just as long as you are able, Mr. Rashleigh," and secondly, it was an economy in fuel. It was distasteful, as he often repeated to Miss Tippett downstairs, to worry about the pence. "My fault, if I may say so, is extravagance." Still, now that people had dropped sending handpainted Christmas cards to each other, it was important not to start the gasfire until the last possible moment. Naturally, he never expected a woman to be punctual, but Agatha, his cousin, was really exasperating; it was often the seventh of the month before she remembered to mail him his little cheque; it made life so difficult.

How hard it was, after an active life, to lie still in the mornings! Up to the previous September there had been sparrows outside, the bobbing tassels of a plane tree, and what he liked to call not cirrus but the nainsook puffets of a cloud. He looked angrily at the black square of paper that kept out the sky. He could have slept for hours after the barrage all night had it not been for the wireless.

It was Eve, and she was quite shameless about it. "I set my alarm for six forty-five and then I roll over and turn on the portable. A bit of swing wakes me up and helps me to get breakfast." In a well-ordered world, girls would not tear down the stairs to business, clattering like a fledgling man-at-arms in a leather coat without even the pretence of a cap on short, smooth hair. It was so different from the picture he remembered, a lawn with croquet colours as the only primitive note (it had been an idea of his to bring out a set of balls in pastel shades), where static figures in silk had watched the game from rustic seats. Nature, clouds, trees, peonies, had moved, just as a painter would have wished, only the people had been quiet, grouped around his wife (and he saw her again for the first time) smiling at the daisies in her hand.

The noise was worse than a dozen roundabouts. "My dear," he had remonstrated gently, "I am an old man, old enough to be your grandfather, but I like gaiety as well as anyone else if it is melodious. How can you bear to listen to such discord?"

"Oh, it has a plan, only it's hard to explain. I do turn it low so as not to disturb you." There had been no question of apology or silence. Forty years ago Eve would have been taught to creep past his door had a necessary errand called her forth early in the morning. It was all a question of money, of greed; dignity had vanished from the world with the passing of Queen Victoria. His wedding day, such a coincidence, had been the birthday of the Queen. People needed to return to the old simplicities, not to say, like Evelyn (perhaps the child had not really meant to be rude), "And whom would you get to carry your scuttle of coal three flights up from the basement? You ought to be thankful that they invented gas fires."

"She's steadier than most," Miss Tippett had commented when he had, no, not complained, there was no vice more intolerable than intolerance, but just mentioned the wireless. "We old folks have got to march with the times." Of course, nobody could accuse Selina of artistic sensibilities. Poor woman, she was one of nature's less successful drawings, a little sketch scribbled on a telephone pad, and he chuckled, of superimposed O's from rump to chin.

Eleven and fourpence, that was the chemist. Agatha grumbled that he took care of himself almost to foolhardiness. "I may as well die from a bomb in my bed as from pneumonia in the shelter." Yet if other people would tramp down to the cellar at night, catching heavy colds, how could he help his bronchitis coming on? This was the week to buy himself some tea. He must have paints, he needed a new camel's-hair brush. There was a book of stamps; three, five, no, he must have ten shillings for the extras. "I can't think, Cousin Horatio, why you have to write so many letters?" Agatha did not know what it felt like to be a lonely old man after thirty years of real domestic happiness. Try as he would, the fuel bill went up and up and he owed Miss Tippett five weeks for the rent. However promptly the monthly cheque arrived, he would need one pound eighteen, no, better say two pounds, to clear everything on his list.

Something would have to be done. There had been a time when he had sold his water-colour sketches for three guineas each. He sat up, pulled his dressing gown about his shoulders and glanced down the names in his address book. Some of them were marked at the side with a cross in red ink, others were underlined in blue. H.I.J. . . . old Mrs. Johnson had been so good to him, perhaps he would try her daughter. He lifted over the little tray with his writing block and settled it on his knees.

"Dear Lady. . ." All he could remember of the Johnson girl was a snapshot that her mother had sent him of a school girl with a big white bow on her hair, standing on the beach. "An old man has few pleasures save remembrance, and I am an old man, seventy-six years of age on my next birthday though my neighbours (kind folk if I may not call them friends) teasingly ask me when I am joining the Home Guard? Turning over my papers yesterday, for I would not wish to cause pain or trouble after I am gone, and Jerry" (no, that was too familiar, he scratched the word out) "and the Germans have paid us Londoners rather too much attention of late, I found this letter from your mother that she wrote to me many years ago about a tiny water colour of mine, *Sunrise over Lon- don Tower*. She had had the delightful thought to send some copies to her friends at Christmas. You will smile, I expect, but lying here at night with the guns going overhead, I could not help wondering what happened to those pictures? I should like to think, vanity, you will say, that my brush was the means of first acquainting some young boy or little girl with the glorious history of their native land."

Horatio shivered. It was chilly writing before breakfast. He pushed the tray aside and pulled up the blankets again, well over his ears. He hoped that Miss Johnson, he had never heard that she had married, was not one of those aggressive women who centred their lives on dogs. Perhaps to be on the safe side, he would add a vague sentence about animals. "I once had the unique privilege of sketching two of the late Queen Victoria's cream ponies for my little nephews." The sentence was pleasantly historical if she happened to prefer the animal world. "Actually, I wanted to ask you, forgive my discursiveness, would you care to have your mother's letter returned to your own keeping? She was so truly thoughtful for others that I have always treasured it and cannot bear that it should be turned over by strangers." He reached a cold hand unwillingly towards the tray again—but it was age, a good sentence had a habit of slipping away like those dear little cirrus clouds he was so fond of, if he did not jot it down. "And you, I fear you must be finding it difficult in these hard times to keep the beautiful garden cared for as you would wish?" He had done a sketch of Mrs. Johnson's hollyhocks one summer. It had been, in fact, the way that their acquaintanceship had begun. She had found him sketching in a neighbouring meadow, had offered him tea and eventually the commission to do her paved walk. The pen scratched, the ink was running dry; it was, no doubt, the cold. "At least you have been spared, I hope, the attentions of our unwelcome visitors. Yours most sincerely, Horatio Rashleigh."

First he must wait a moment for his chilly hands to thaw under the blanket, then he would get up and light the fire. After breakfast he would make a clean copy of the letter and write, perhaps, a postcard to Agatha. It was no morning to be tardy if he were going to buy his tea; unless he reached Mr. Dobbie's shop by a quarter to ten, there would be no opportunity for a chat.

Horatio rubbed his hands together, impatient for an activity that the icy room denied. His seascape seemed to reproach him with its galleons and billowing clouds. He had hung it directly over what had once been the fireplace but was now, alas, blocked in except for the chalklike pipes of the gas stove. Perhaps it was, as they had teased him in his youth, a shade too influenced by Turner, but it was his own spirit that was in every line of Drake's ship. The firm precise lines of the rigging stood out as if drawn in sepia, gallantly, under the clouds and flame of the Spanish hull. A prophecy perhaps: "We are all now, Miss Evelyn, Drakes in our own small way," to which the child had replied (these modern schools, what did they care about the past?), "Well, if the Ministry of Food continues its wilful course we could do with some more ducks."

Forty years ago the picture had hung proudly in the Academy. Not, naturally, in a good light, but then not all whom the Muses called were able to withstand the intoxication of success. If his peers had passed him by, Art, itself, had not failed him. It was better to bring beauty to untutored eyes, and now that he was an old man he could say this convincingly, than to hang bleakly in a gallery before a dozen students and halfhearted visitors tramping from room to room to while away the time. His ships had been the gay cover for *First Steps to History, Part II.* They had been a calendar, even a jigsaw puzzle. Some might laugh, like that fellow Dale who sneered about "coloured photographs" just because he had never learned to draw but made splotches in red and black with his thumb that he called *Abstract No. 7.* What the world needed was not machinery but penitence, a return to apprenticeship, to straight lines and "taking pains." Why, this war was raging because people wanted to make haste, were shoddy, indifferent to detail, selfishly avid of some temporary laurel, unlike the anonymous craftsmen who had spent a lifetime on some obscure corner of a cathedral wall. "The artist abhors engines," he had said stiffly to Evelyn only the night before. "And what about Leonardo and his flying machines?" she had joked; it had surprised him that she knew a painter's name. "Da Vinci," he had rebuked her, "was a genius, but there is an element about his work, I except the *Mona Lisa*, that we can only describe as, well...bitter." He had not cared, though the young women of today talked about things that hardly entered even a man's head, to mention the unfortunate circumstances of Leonardo's family life. "Someday," he had suggested, for you never knew, some chance words might reveal the treasures of the spirit to the young, "you must come with me to the National Gallery. There is a blue in a Fra Angelico there that is the absolute colour of the Tuscan sky." "I'll be so glad, Mr. Rashleigh, when peace comes that I'll do anything"; and he had recalled with a start that the pictures, of course, were transferred to the country for the duration.

After the war. Horatio shivered suddenly, less with cold than with hatred. Those vandals! All his life he had been resisting some mysterious power, and there it was in the sky with its shrieking engines (Grandfather had been right to predict the doom of the world at his first sight of a locomotive) tearing up moral values, lustily destroying homes. (Miss Tippett had told him yesterday that men and women were sleeping together in the shelters, without even a screen.) If one were seventy-six, every moment counted. There were no brave words about death except when one was young. Suppose he were too ailing, when it stopped, to go to the National Gallery again? Suppose Agatha should really be unable to send him his allowance, his hand fail, his last clients abandon calendars? It was dreary enough to be an old man and have no soul to comfort him without these fiendish noises and the Government cutting down his butter. Let them keep his meat if they wanted, but he had never tasted margarine, poor as he had been, and he was not going to begin now. Perhaps he felt so gloomy because he was restless and the room was cold; it did not do to resign one's self to melancholy. Very cautiously he sat up, pulled a second dressing gown about his shoulders, and felt for his slippers. An icy draught blew under the badly fitting door. Most people of his age would be stiff, half bedridden; if he did not leap up, at least he was as agile as he had been at sixty. He filled the kettle, set a match to the gas fire.

It was too chilly to open the window, and the black paper sternly obscured the light. The sputtering flame scorched Horatio's legs but he dared not leave its comfort. Getting up had never been a problem in the old days when he had crept out at dawn with his easel to watch the cows advancing with slow, comfortable steps over multitudinous little flowers. Those were the hours that he would choose to live again; how one had tossed away one's riches! For the very sky that was symbolical of peace, of heaven, was desecrated by barbarian beasts flinging missiles at the roof, at his own head! He had seemed to be walking in a wood the night before, remarkably like the little copse near his early home, when from nowhere something had sprung at him with a great noise—then he had wakened to the sirens. Oh, why were people destructive? They had pulled down the windmill he had painted, they laughed at his lace valentines; it reminded him of that terrible moment in his boyhood that he had never quite forgotten, when a horde of shouting, older boys with feathers and wooden tomahawks had sprung on him from behind trees and knocked him, sprawling, into the moss that had been his castle.

He would feel better, he always did, after he had had a cup of tea.

2

SELINA TIPPETT, WHO ought to have been called Madge, trotted down the stairs. Ruby, she surmised, would be late; she always was on Thursday, a day nobody at the Warming Pan had time to stand around and chat with her. It was astonishing how the draught got under the windows; the corridors ("so much lighter than you usually find in London houses") were hardly an advantage in winter. A solitary china plate hanging on the wall looked as if its fragile colours were not worn but frozen out of it. Undoubtedly Angelina had got her chill running up from the hot kitchen to see that the beds had been made. If I were not in business, Selina thought, I should certainly wear mittens; and she saw herself suddenly, as clearly as if Mr. Rashleigh had painted the scene in a calendar, standing outside her father's door one Christmas Eve and pulling a pair of grey, woolly, fingerless gloves out of a packet with "to Miss Roly Poly" in Cook's writing on the tiny, attached label. Mittens

…they were mixed up with snowmen and her mother's displeasure. "Selina, your hair ribbon is untied; I will not have you playing with those rough boys." Dear me, she frightened herself by saying the words aloud, how the world has changed since I was ten. Changed for the better, too, in spite of the raids. Nobody questioned a girl like Evelyn about her friends, she went unchallenged to her work in the mornings; even, in peacetime, might aspire to a post abroad.

"Good morning, Timothy." The shop blinds were down, of course, for they did not open until ten, but the floor was swept and the tables replaced in rows. "Good morning, madam, it was a terribly noisy night." Timothy flicked his duster over the office desk and chair and waited with his permanent inborn sadness for comfort. "Yes, if we listen to the Prime Minister we shall have worse to endure before it's over"—the people, poor dears, were being magnificent but it only encouraged them to lose their nerve if you let them discuss the horrors. "It was a land mine, madam, at the corner of the Square; the milkman told me it 'ad 'it two empty 'ouses. Fairly blazing, it was; at eleven last night, I could see to read the time as plain as day."

"Indeed, we must be thankful that there was not more damage." These extraordinary events needed, Selina thought, a new and quite other vocabulary, but morale—that was the important thing; it was the difference that severed England, more than the Channel did, from the Continent. "The best thing to do, Angelina," she had repeated this twice to her partner the previous evening, "is to go on as if everything were absolutely normal. The staff copies us unconsciously and in that way we are influencing not just Ruby, Timothy, and the customers but perhaps hundreds of people." For if clients came in to lunch and went off cheerfully afterwards, they, in turn, would affect their relatives and their maids. It was inspiring really, especially on such a cold, dreary morning, to think how much one solitary woman could do in defence of her native land.

In wartime, however, it was impossible to be gay or brave for long. Selina glanced at her desk; there was a pile of letters stacked on the worn leather, and the contents were bound to be unpleasant. Some people, she supposed, really liked their post; news came from strange, far-off places or spoke of acquaintances amusingly. A letter ought to be the sharing of a life, but now correspondence had come to mean answering stupid questions after the day's work or pointing out an error in the gas account. The postman himself was Fate with a large F, for at nine or eleven or four he might bring the papers that she was sure to receive one day: either they must pay the arrears of rent or the landlord would have regretfully (she saw the polite, pinched phrase) to give them notice.

There was a circular from the Ministry of Food. Butler's, of course, wanted something on account, they always did at the beginning of the month. She planned to take them methodically but it was no use; she had to run them through her hands, anxiously, until she was sure that the dreaded white envelope stamped with *Private* had not arrived. Only when she was certain of the landlord's silence could she begin to slit them open with her pet paper knife, the one with a carnelian handle made from pebbles she had once picked up on the beach, and begin to arrange them for reply.

Omens... if one let one's self believe in them, she would say that something was about to happen. Selina turned, not the pages of the ledger with the fish account nor the note with indecipherable signature, but a great photograph album of the Warming Pan. She would never forget an evening when she had faced Miss Humphries in a dreary Bournemouth hotel. The coffee had been cold and powdery for the third evening in succession, but she had seen herself, exactly as if in a dream, walking down a street past an empty shop.

Tearooms had had a special meaning for Selina. She associated them with freedom. Only those people, she thought, who lived obedience for six and a half days of the week knew what liberty was. From Friday morning until the following Thursday noon she read aloud, matched wool, pushed the bath chair, or dreamed whilst "poor Miss Humphries" slept, but on Thursday afternoon she strolled out, dressed as she herself chose, to meet some friend at the local confectioner's. They discussed their "posts," the Church, the Court, the necessity to keep in touch with fashion but not to be dominated by it, and the food. Her budget permitted her to spend only one and six, but such a sum offered vast possibilities of choice. She could have, for example, buttered toast or scones, a piece of plum cake, a tartlet, or some sandwiches. There was no temptation in expensive foreign-looking pastry. Selina collected teashops as wealthier people tasted wines. Sometimes she had taken the train into the country, ostensibly to pick bluebells, really to try out a recommended "Farmhouse Tea." In one place the butter was good, another excelled in crumpets but the cakes were soggy; she had never found "the toast, the temperature, and the tea," as she paraphrased to Angelina gaily, all together. Then, that evening when everybody in the sombre hall except herself had been well over seventy, she had seen it suddenly, complete even to its name, the perfect meeting place, not smart but homelike, with gay primrose china and tiny, polished tables.

"No, Selina, people always lose money on them," Angelina had insisted. It had happened to be her free evening and they had been sitting together in her bedroom with the door open, in case Miss Humphries should call. "Of course, but nobody ever runs them properly; it's the little things that they always forget, but men are so insensitive." That, at least, was a point upon which they were both agreed. "Yes, but as often as not they are started by women, the fat and fussy type. Now look at that place we went to last Saturday; the tea was filthy and the crumpets stank of margarine and there wasn't a male in the place."

It was Angelina's way, her friend had thought, to oppose all projects not originated by herself. There were days during the next year when Selina almost talked herself into believing that the Warming Pan existed, whilst it had, all the time, the quality of pure dream until Miss Humphries had died, had left her unexpectedly three hundred pounds, and she had walked one morning into the ideal, empty shop.

The seven years telescoped themselves into one, for there had not been a day when she had not felt vibrantly, excitedly alive. She had been frightened at first, no, never when they had actually opened, only during those early moments when they had signed the lease, engaged the waitresses, and she had wondered if she would be able to pay the bills. She remembered now looking up at the newly distempered walls and saying to Angelina, "But will customers ever come?" It had been so astonishing when the first ones had arrived, a flustered lady with parcels and two quarrelling little boys. The second arrival, she had recognized her immediately, had been a governess. "Look, Angelina," she had whispered, "there is somebody there, what must I do?" Yet it had been sheer gaiety, almost a pretense of being frightened; she had behaved as if she had been for twenty years, not a lady companion with excellent references, but the manageress of a smart hotel. Everything had happened just "as if it had been meant"; for Sarah, the assistant, whose help had been invaluable at the start, had married and left the place indisputably under Selina's control. Angelina looked after the staff and the purchases, but her heart was really with the courses that she was always taking to improve, as she said, "the future of us women."

"Number Seven is leaving this morning," Timothy remarked. He had emptied the pails of water in the kitchen and had come back to spread his wet cloths on the radiator to dry. Strictly speaking, this was forbidden but Ruby made such a fuss if he cluttered the kitchen up that they pretended not to notice provided that he cleared them away by ten o'clock. "I saw the van draw up as I came down the street. Looks to me as if between the bombs and the people running to the country there won't be a London left."

"I read somewhere," Selina said severely, "that it will take three years and a half to lay the city in ruins." It might be statistically correct but she could not help agreeing inwardly with Timothy, who looked the essence of gloom, that this was poor comfort after a noisy night.

"You can never believe what you read in them papers," Timothy objected, appealing to her with damp, brown, spaniel eyes—it was the only phrase to use about him, if it did sound bookish.

"Well, we are not going to give the Germans the satisfaction of making us neglect our jobs; I think that inside handle could do with a rub this morning; it's the dust, I know, from the explosions." His glum uneasiness was irritating to the nerves.

Selina was just as aware as Timothy that every person gone from the district meant one less possible customer. Those prewar days of January sales when they had served a hundred lunches in a morning had vanished as surely and inevitably as the snowballing moments of her first mittens. To think that she had ever grumbled about the smallness of their oven! Now it was not a question of putting savings in a bank for their old age but of meeting current expenses; she could not even think about the overdue rent. Of course, Selina would have liked to say to the porter, don't you worry, when you can't work for us any more there will be a pension waiting; but then someone would have to promise the same thing to Miss Tippett herself, and she could not see the landlord, for instance, offering them anything but notice.

How strange life was! They fulfilled a need in the neighbourhood; they were, as Selina often remarked, a cross between a village shop and the family doctor. They found old Mrs. Holmes a dressmaker, delivered messages to deaf Miss Clark. People rushed in to telephone; if they were favourites, to dump their parcels. They used them unthinkingly, she reflected, taking up a letter with an indecipherable signature, "... and I must have left the gloves on the window ledge, you could not help noticing them, they were an *almost new* brown knitted pair with blue dots on the gauntlets and besides your restaurant I was only at Barlow's and the chemist's and a cinema. Please send them to me registered and I will pay you back the postage the next time I drop in." That must come from the angular woman who always grumbled about her table. Yes, the Warming Pan was useful, whatever Angelina might say. Her partner had behaved so oddly ever since she had gone to this new political course; it had been so much easier when she had taken up Eastern philosophy, for then she had made an effort to control her temper. Now she was scornful of the customers, called them the "stupid bourgeoisie," when they were really such nice people. It made life very confusing.

"Timothy," perhaps he would cheer up if she talked to him a little, "have you seen a pair of brown gloves anywhere? A customer says she dropped a pair here the . . ."—she looked at the date and at the calendar—"the day before yesterday."

"Brown gloves, madam?" He was antagonistic immediately, as if she thought that he might have taken them. "There's this one from last week." He held up an object from the *Found* basket with a large hole in one worn, black finger.

"No, that's not it. She says brown, and new. Probably she left them somewhere else." Instinctively, Selina treated all customers as she had humoured a succession of Miss Humphries. "In the bus, I expect."

"It's surprising what people do leave in vehicles," Timothy commented mysteriously, "'specially in trams." He shook his leather and, looking at the doorknob with an almost hypnotized stare, started to flick away the dust.

Selina walked over to the window and began, through sheer habit, to arrange the trays of cakes. With the shortage of eggs and currants, all experiments had gone. She had prided herself before that nowhere in all the district had good standard things and so much variety been united. There had always been nicely browned crumpets and thick gingerbread, rock cakes and buns, the sort of food people wanted after a hard day or some hours of freedom too precious to waste on lunch. Certain afternoons (she remembered Miss Humphries), all she could have swallowed were teacakes with just the right amount of butter. Then there were other moments, after days indoors perhaps because of an east wind that caught the old lady's chest, when a piece of seed cake, made from Grandmother's mixture, had brought back blackberry days and times when lessons were the only threat to a placid routine of life. She looked sadly at the meagre row; there was something stinted and miserly about it. It was not the bombs that distressed her, awful as the noise was, so much as the lack of loaded trays to make up for the horrors of the night. She hated ration cards, less because she wanted more food herself than because they were a symbol of some poverty of spirit. They reminded her of vegetarian teachers with cramped ideas. If Angelina would only eat more, she would be less restless and talk less strangely. How detestable the propaganda of the Food Ministry was, with the emphasis upon oatmeal and raw carrots; were they not fighting for an England of plenty, for that older England of sirloins of beef and mountains of cheddar cheese?

It looked so cold out too, raw and winterly, and there was poor Mr. Rashleigh trotting up the street in his worn-out overcoat. Selina was thankful that Angelina was not there to see him. "That dreadful old man," she would say, rapping the desk with her pencil. "But, Angelina, we can't turn him out, he has nowhere to go." She dreaded seeing again the contemptuous shrug of her partner's shoulders. "In a properly organized Britain there would be places for such people." Perhaps it would be a good idea, though a little gloomy, to have homes for all the old. Still, as it appeared that Britain was not organized—"and, you know, dear, elderly people, and I have had so much experience with them, do get dreadfully jealous of each other"—it cost them very little to let him remain upstairs. Nobody would take an attic these days, anyhow. After all, when Angelina spoke of her "new England" it was always of a world of young people swimming or riding motorcycles, and she was not really mechanical, no, indeed, though Selina hardly liked to tell her so; her colleague could not even hang a picture up without help.

Selina turned back towards her desk. The room was warm and gay, but for the first time she saw clearly a possible *To Let* sign at the windows and deserted, empty corridors. As long as I have a pair of hands and work (how often she had said this) nothing matters. Yet it was not mere selfishness now to be afraid; there were Timothy and Ruby, even the furniture itself that had been cleaned and polished for so many years. There are worse things than war, she caught herself thinking, though this, of course, was the result of war. Perhaps the bombing would stop and people would come back again or a factory would be opened; perhaps even some morning they would wake up and find that there was an armistice? "Timothy," she called, "don't forget to move the cloths from the radiator before we open the shop."

3

THE SHOP WAS SMALL, a few doors from the Warming Pan, and so inconspicuous that strangers, unless they knew, dismissed it as a warehouse. There was a dingy, Victorian quality about the windows, and the white canisters standing on the counter reminded Horatio, as he stepped inside, of an apothecary's den. He longed to run his fingers over the blue spirals down their sides or sniff the lids; they must hold spices, he thought, as well as coffee. One expected the owner to be eccentric and bad-tempered, and sometimes Mr. Dobbie was both; at a first glance he looked like an innkeeper, but to the initiate the passivity of his oblong face suggested tea and china.

Horatio had timed his visit exactly. Jim, the boy, was still polishing the handles of various doors. In ten minutes shoppers would arrive, from real households where they had a wad of ration books and bought not in miserable ounces but in pounds. He looked forward to this chat, for it was a contact with the life he missed so sorely now that his wife was dead and there were no more Sunday suppers where his pupils ("Quite Bohemian, my dear, from all ranks and classes, but art—art is unity") were welcomed.

"Good morning, Mr. Dobbie, and how are you this morning? You had rather a noisy night of it, I am afraid."

"Noisy! We were up till two with that fire in the Square." A ledger banged as if its owner would like, with such a gesture, to smash up the war.

"Ah, yes, incendiaries. Well, well, to think I didn't hear them, but my hearing's not so good as it used to be; age, Mr. Dobbie, age, but it's uphill work quarrelling with time!"

"Quite." Mr. Dobbie stared at the empty packing cases that cut off most of the light. "Take the mat outside and shake it, Jim, we must try to get rid of that dust."

"Sometimes I feel that to be hard of hearing these days is a blessing in disguise."

"Certainly it has its compensations. And what can I do for you this morning, Mr. Rashleigh?"

It was an inauspicious day, Horatio reflected; Mr. Dobbie was tired. "Why, the same as usual, with Whitehall's permission." He handed over his book. "All this rationing must be very bad for business."

"Bad! It's ruinous. And to think," Mr. Dobbie's forehead wrinkled into as many lines as the Chinese characters above him, "to think that the Conservative Party did this to me. Lied to us, they did, lied to us… and I voted for them at the last election!" Dobbie could bear any stupidity ill, least of all his own.

"Don't say that, Mr. Dobbie, I am sure Mr. Baldwin meant

well even if he was misinformed."

"Misinformed! Misinformed, Mr. Rashleigh, is hardly the word to use. What do we pay the Government for, I should like to know, with good money taken from your pocket and mine, if they go and deliberately mislead us? They knew—half a pound of second-quality breakfast, Jim, for the gentleman— they knew what those Germans were arming for; and where are they now? Helping us to put out fires and freeze in the dark? Oh, no, most of them are in Canada, safe and warm and toasting their toes at a log fire whilst we, who were idiotic enough to vote for them, catch bronchitis and pay for Spitfires." He snatched the funnel from Jim's hand and poured tea through it into a twist of paper.

"I have heard," Horatio ventured timidly, "that in Canada they have radiators."

"Doesn't matter, they've feathered their nests all right. It's a shame," he added kindly, "that a gentleman of your age can't have a pot of tea when he chooses without having to count the leaves."

"Thank you, Mr. Dobbie, it is a little hard, especially, if I may say so, for one who has a palate for the beverage. Better a cup a day of the best, though, than four out of some nameless packet." He hoped Mr. Dobbie had not noticed how many months it was since he had been able to afford his favourite blend.

"You are right, you are supremely right; now which was it that Mrs. Rashleigh used to come in for at Christmas?" Dobbie glanced admiringly up at the jars above his head. "This one, wasn't it?" He pointed to a canister.

"Yes, that was Margaret's gift to me for years. Such a bitter loss," he sighed, "I was thinking of her only this morning."

"Quite, quite," Dobbie answered vaguely; he was a bachelor and proud of it. "There's a lot to be said for the single life, all the same."

There was something about Dobbie, Horatio reflected, that stamped him as commercial. He was like—Rashleigh could not think of the term, then all at once the memory surged back to him—a big, vulgar trader selling blankets on the cover of a book of Indian stories, the one, he smiled to think of it now, that had frightened him so as a child. A simple mind could smash itself against that broad, impervious smile. Not that Dobbie was a bad fellow, he knew his place and kept to it, but he was a materialist. Imagine trying to explain to him the meaning of the word "ideal"!

Jim kicked a pail at the back of the counter and looked up guiltily at the noise. He flicked his duster over an already shiny shelf. "See the grinder's all right," Dobbie snapped, reopening the ledger. A merchant was busy enough these days without wasting time in idle conversation. He glanced at the clock. "Funny how much you miss a night's sleep," he grumbled, thinking of the glorious moment when he could cross the road and sit down in front of a pint of beer.

Horatio put a half crown on the counter deliberately, though he had some change in his pocket. The longer that he could remain in the warm shop the better; the hardwood crates with their exotic labels, French or Chinese, suggested the ships that he had sketched for fifty years. Why, he could see the *Solent* in front of him again, the short blue waves slapping the little tugs and beyond them, an etching rather than a water colour, for the lines were so exquisite, the bow of a liner,

Asia-bound.

"I think I must be due for my tea." Horatio started, for he had not heard the door click, and looked up, a little suspiciously, at the grey-haired stranger beside him.

"Yes, Colonel Ferguson," Dobbie thumbed over a dozen dirty pages fastened with a clip, "you deposited your coupons, didn't you?" He extracted a paper and looked at it. "Half a pound. Will you take it today?"

"Please. You had a bad time last night, I am afraid?" "I miss my sleep. We had quite a blaze in the Square." "It's marvellous to me the way that people stand it." "Well, as one of our Ministers remarked the other day, *what else is there to do? It isn't war, though, it's murder.*" Dobbie blew his nose violently, an aggressively white handkerchief floating like a flag against the dust. "Anything more I can do for you, Mr. Rashleigh?" he inquired, for Horatio was still fumbling with his change.

"No, no, thank you." Rashleigh slid the coins into his pocket. If he had still been able to afford the six and twopenny China, no tradesman would have dared dismiss him in such a manner. Colonel Ferguson! He gazed icily at his neighbour whilst buttoning his coat. Just because the man had a military title, though with his blue, far-off-looking eyes he seemed more of a sailor, Dobbie wanted to clear the coast, no doubt, before handing him something from "under the counter." That was the worst of war, the artists suffered first. Horatio turned, almost knocking over the scarlet canister painted with pansies that held a ball of string, and stamped into the street. He would lose himself, and that was something these other people could not do, painting a petite water colour in case Miss Johnson should reply to his letter, an impression of the

Golden Hind perhaps or else *Rose Cottage* with his dear white ducks waddling towards the pond.

"A cold morning," Ferguson remarked, watching the merchant knot two pieces of string together; "somehow it would be easier to put up with these disturbances if we had some sun."

"Everyone to their fancy, sir." Dobbie sifted the tea into a bag and shook it. "Give me a sharp, December day myself." His plump neck bulged out of its collar as he turned towards the cash register. "That will be three and a penny, or shall I book it to your account?"

Unlike Horatio, Colonel Ferguson preferred to shop as expeditiously as possible. He put down the exact amount, thrust his parcel into his pocket, and with a brisk "Good morning" left, closing the door carefully behind him. Fire fighting must be a new experience for a man like Dobbie, and he did not look as if he were a fellow who was used to discomfort. He was making a good job of it all the same, the Colonel thought; it was wonderful the way these wardens had tackled the crisis. He crossed the street and turned up towards the park. It would be deserted, but he meant to round the Serpentine for it would be fatal to give up exercise just because this raw, damp, miserable climate took away the heart for it. He had never had to force himself to walk in Lausanne; there he had known the hills from the first wild clump of chicory up to the highest hepaticas, but today he would be as shivery when he got indoors as he was now, having just had breakfast. It was not age, he could swear it was not age. Why, he had felt as gay and young in Lausanne as if he had been fourteen, with life—and the East—still in front of him.

England had changed. It was less familiar, certainly less friendly, than the Continent. There were still the old colours in the fabric; people stood up nightly to the raids as if they were merely thunderstorms, but there was a new, ugly, bureaucratic class without guts and without what he called "empire imagination." They laughed at his fifty years of service as if he had been some petty tax collector. He was still fuming over yesterday's interview. "I don't understand, sir, why you returned to London," the official had said, pursing his lips as if he nibbled a pencil permanently. "You have been domiciled abroad ever since you left India and you are well over military age." Colonel Ferguson had not even troubled to reply, "To offer my services." After half a dozen young men in as many different Ministries had turned him down in varying tones of boredom and icy politeness, the logical part of his mind was saying "Why?" to himself.

It would be different this afternoon. Finally Ferguson had unearthed Harris, his old chief. With Departments evacuated all over the countryside, his letter had gone to a dozen places before it had reached its destination. Harris himself was marooned in Yorkshire but had sent him an introduction to a London colleague who would be sure, he wrote, "to fix you up at once." Ferguson was seeing the man at three, and tomorrow, or at latest next week, he would be back, surely, in harness?

There were no children in the park, not even an old maid with her dog. Along the entire row there were only himself and a French soldier, walking towards him, looking frozen and miserable. For a moment Colonel Ferguson felt tempted to speak, to say, "I don't feel at home here myself," but his French was rusty and the fellow might not have understood him. How they must miss the sun, the funny shutters with the paint scratched off, not with nails but with light, the clusters of . . . what did they call it . . . *glycines*, that were so formal in spite of their abundance, and reminded him of grapes in an architectural drawing. It was all very well to make speeches, but imagine the landing that these men had had, struggling up the salt-stained steps of some West Country port, with everything lost, no news, and nobody to welcome them. Two wars in a single generation asked too much of any race.

The trees reminded Ferguson of the brooms in a shop that he had just passed. It was not their stiffness, for they were soft against the autumn sky, but their tiny, bristling edges made just the same patterns as the brushes against the glass window. A piece of parachute silk fluttered from a branch near the explosive circle of a new crater. Patches of grass were corroded as if by acid, a piece of broken railing stuck out of the earth. The whole landscape had the bare, haunted loneliness of the moors in *Lear*; only a fretful succession of necessary acts, eating, sleeping, getting warm, differentiated life from nightmare.

It was strange how impressions returned, as if they were no isolated events but had separate echoes vibrating along memory. Lausanne was a blur in his mind; it was coming home, that final day in Paris, that he could not get out of his head. He saw himself (it must be meeting that French soldier) walking up the Champs Élysées under absurd catkin-coloured little clouds whilst the different faces brought back the journeys of his life as if it were farewell, not to France only but to all the harbours of a long experience.

Ferguson had had the whole afternoon in front of him and no friends to visit. There had been fewer taxis but nearly as many cars, most of them unmistakably civilian, racing powerfully towards the Bois. The wind had been sharp in spite of the April colours, and because he was a little tired after the long night in the train he had drifted into a spiral of people waiting outside a cinema. He liked a good picture now and again though it was hard work to find one. For a moment he had seen an earlier Paris, carriages drawn by grey and roan horses, children in pinafores holding the hands of governesses in big, feathered hats. Nothing changed really, he had thought, except environment; it was easier to develop some years than others. There had been the usual bourgeois couple in the queue, the wife in black, with a square, shiny handbag tucked under her arm as she clung to her plump husband's rather rumpled sleeve. Why was it that French materials seemed to crush immediately? *Froissé*, it was a better word than creased but unsuited to the texture of English, either language or cloth. They were discussing the price of butter, the Colonel thought, though it was easy to miss a phrase after the leisurely sung Vaudois. A Senegalese was staring at the poster whilst a soldier slouched beside them in a grease-stained tunic and the worst military boots that he had ever seen. Of course, the French could improvise, but wasn't there also something to be said for English smartness? Perhaps he had listened too much to his neighbours in Lausanne; they were always showing him photographs of sunburnt faces under steel helmets. There was one picture of tanks crawling round a road in a gigantic question mark that had haunted his mind for months. Morale was more important than machinery and yet, Colonel Ferguson looked up suddenly at another ribbon of silk flapping beside a dead, solitary leaf, in that moment of memory he had seen personified in a single soldier the story of an end of France.

It was too cold, too lonely; even if the war ended in an hour, there would always be a rift, a sense of loss. History repeated itself, but in each age there was something as ephemeral as these autumn reds and russets that no reconstruction could replace. The bright ochre leaves rolled away into the gutters, and under a scarred tree that had half its roots in the air the pathway was littered with small branches and green twigs. Death is not dissolution, the Colonel thought, turning towards the park gates; it is the moment when humanity needs our services no longer. He must not be foolish, however, just because the morning was so desolate; there were years of work in him still if he could only get a job. An old lady, waiting at the corner, looked up at the sky; the sirens began again, shaking the air and picking each other up among the buildings until he thought of wolves, answering from hill to hill. "That's the second alert this morning," the conductor grumbled as he boarded a calm but half-empty bus. "Wouldn't you think, sir, that they could find something better to do?"

It was possible to catch a glimpse of the street through small diamonds cut out of the splinter netting across the windows, but they altered the perspective strangely and gave an illusion of speed. Ferguson's neighbour went on reading his paper. He had read it, no doubt, for twenty years in the same manner and, raid or no raid, the habits of a lifetime were not easily broken. An old lady in a brown fur jacket that hung shapelessly to her waist clasped a hamper containing not parcels but a Pekinese. The bow of her grey felt hat stuck up like an ear. "They have got some really good bath towels, dear, at Barlow's," she chattered, "an absolute bargain. I got a dozen yesterday, and three little striped bathing ones for Woggles. Darling," she glanced at the black rose resting on the rim of the basket, "he will get his toes so wet."

"But do you think in these days it is right to buy anything?" Her friend's face was almost green with terror and she gripped a black handbag tightly with both hands.

"Of course. You should be a fatalist like me. Besides, if you are really nervous, you can always send a trunk to the country."

"I wonder you haven't evacuated Woggles."

"He doesn't seem to mind. If it is very noisy, he barks." "Pekes always were good watchdogs in spite of their size, but do you suppose he realizes the danger?"

The gunfire slackened in the distance. "Barlow's," the conductor shouted. Most of the passengers stood up. How extraordinary people were, Ferguson thought, getting up with the others, armoured against defeat with this sublime stupidity. They had ignored all warnings only to be ready to fight to the last dog for some unpredictable reason of their own that, born here though he was, he was unable to analyse. Woggles, released from his basket, sniffed a piece of shell and his mistress smacked him. An old man went on gravely painting white lines along a row of sandbags. Nobody had even thought of going to a shelter; and, looking up at the grey, dismal sky, Ferguson was almost sorry for the Germans.

4

You never know
who's
listening!

ADELAIDE SPENSER PAUSED in front of Barlow's plate-glass windows less to inspect the carpets than to admire her hat. It was essential today not to lower one's standards. Thomas had been quite impossible last night; but then, poor dear, though he would not admit it, he did not really like raids. He had been so rude at dinner that Kate had given notice and it had taken hours of patient listening to her grievances before Adelaide had contrived to smooth things over. As reward she had spent the last hour trying on models that sat upon forlorn stands, simply crying to be bought and worn. Normally she would never have purchased anything so obvious as this tricolour ribbon, but in an autumn when people seemed to welcome drabness with a sort of gaiety, the bright blue and scarlet cheered her up. If her husband were to accuse her of extravagance she would quote the words to him that he had used about stocking up the cellar: "It will be double the price that it is now, next year."

The central display was not a still life of those amazing waxlike figures with impossible dresses and a parchment smile but a large piece of glass covered with torn and dirty netting. "In spite of a bomb dropping in the immediate neighbourhood," a notice said circumspectly, "there was no splintering." The shop windows themselves had been fitted with a device resembling a spokeless wheel. The bright green gloves arranged above a minute black handbag looked infinitely brave or absurdly anachronistic according to one's mood. A driver put his brakes on suddenly and she looked up at the screech, thinking that it was another warning; but the skies were clear and the sound passed into the ordinary rumble of wheels.

It was a good thing that she had asked her sister-in-law to meet her at the Warming Pan, Adelaide thought, as she crossed the road and turned into a side street. Poor Alice never knew, with her diets and her ideas, whether she was eating toast or the plump breast of a partridge. Anything other than "good plain food" would be wasted on her, so difficult in these days when luxuries could be obtained with ease but eggs had almost disappeared. She must remember to stop at Parke's on the way home and get some more canned fruit. Mrs. Spenser had begun stocking her larder directly after Munich when any fool could have seen that there was bound to be a war. Alice had had conscientious scruples. Adelaide could still see her sister-in-law's blue eyes, which must have been faded before she was out of school, and hear the excited voice, "Oh, Adelaide, isn't Mr. Chamberlain *wonderful?* I *knew* if we prayed enough we should have peace."

"How does being an ostrich save one from disaster?" Adelaide had wanted to reply, having already ordered sixty pounds of marmalade; but arguments were bad for the complexion and the best way to deal with relatives, she had found out by long experience, was to sit quietly, say nothing, and treat herself to a good dinner afterwards.

The marmalade had proved invaluable. Mrs. Spenser had locked it up in the tall cupboard where she had formerly kept her summer clothes, doling out an occasional pot as if it were gold in substance as well as colour. She had bartered five pounds of it for eggs; it made such a difference both to Thomas and his temper if he had his usual breakfast. Yes, it was amusing to reflect that she was probably responsible for his recent promotion. When his colleagues had been evacuated, he had realized so well the horrors of a country billet that he had fought for a transfer and got his Department. Dear Thomas, he was so proud, he thought it was merit!

There were no cakes in the Warming Pan window and only a small tray of pastries on the counter inside the entrance. The numerous empty seats were a sign of war. Formerly it had been so crowded at noon that shoppers had often had to share a table. Adelaide glanced round, picked out the best place by the wall, and then, knowing that Alice would be late, she opened her newspaper at the crossword page and felt in her handbag for a pencil. The only people in the room were Mr. Rashleigh, whom she knew by sight, and a few shopgirls. Normally Miss Tippett discouraged them, because it was rather distracting to sit down for a cup of coffee beside the woman who had just been fitting you with shoes; but today everybody was welcome. This part of the West End was absolutely deserted. Seeing a regular customer at last, Selina trotted up, all smiles.

"Good morning, Mrs. Spenser, so you haven't left London? I was beginning to be afraid that you had joined 'the great migration' yourself."

"Dear me, no! I always preferred a florist's window to a garden, and I positively hate cows. I suppose the war has made a lot of difference to you? How are things getting on?"

The correct answer should have been "Splendidly, thank you," but Selina hesitated, in spite of her resolution. "We mustn't grumble, of course, but the times are a little trying."

"Unnecessarily so," Adelaide's voice was firmer than she intended, "when you think that we could have stopped the whole affair in 1933 with a thousand British policemen."

"It was hard to know what to do for the best," Selina ventured cautiously. It was an unbreakable rule, always be neutral with customers. "But I am sure that the Government meant well," she added loyally, "all of us wanted peace."

But it isn't a static thing, Adelaide longed to reply; it isn't the name of a virtue to be copied out in coloured inks and hung in a school hall. A louse is no respecter of persons; think what a single dirty basement can do to a town. Cause and effect, however, would be rather beyond Selina's comprehension. "How is your partner?" she inquired instead. Angelina always had such a smart haircut. "I missed her as I came in. I hope she hasn't left you?"

"Oh, no," this time Miss Tippett could reply without hesitation, "I really don't know what I should do without her. She is so very good with the Food Office. I suppose all these regulations are necessary," she glanced up tentatively because Mrs. Spenser's husband was in some Ministry, "but I am so stupid, somehow, about forms."

"Well, they have to find work for all these women volunteers to do, and besides, they love adding another straw to the burden of us poor taxpayers," though it would be much simpler to tip the butcher, Adelaide thought—and how such a suggestion would shock the Tippett. "I'm waiting for my sister-in-law," she added, "she went dashing off to the country last June and... it does amuse me... this is the first time she has ventured up, even for the day."

"I read in the papers this morning that it would take three and a half years of the present raids to demolish London; but I don't know, sometimes I wonder if we shall have any customers left by the end of the month." Selina could not help her anxiety showing, but Mrs. Spenser might have a little information. "Do you imagine that the Ministries will set up new departments? They took over Barlow's in the last war, one of their buyers told me, and had over four hundred clerks there." It would mean a steady flow of lunches even if they had to provide a cheaper type of meal.

"Hardly in London at the moment." It was extraordinary, Adelaide thought; one should not exaggerate but the poor old Tippett seemed to have no sense of personal danger. "Still, we have reached our level in this district, all the nervous people must have left."

It was another rule, never talk too long to a customer, who might get bored or, worse, too communicative. With a final "Well, we are glad to see you here again," Selina started back towards her pay desk, stopping to greet Rashleigh as she passed him.

Horatio had his special seat and had made an art out of taking an hour for lunch. He was delighted with the invaders; shopgirls chattered so gaily and had such smart clothes. "Don't bother about my order, Ruby," he would say, "serve these young ladies first. They are in a hurry and I am a vassal to Time. . . ." Then he would hand the menu card to them with a smile and a little bow, hoping that they would speak to him, which they never did. He wished, he could never say how much he wished, that his dear wife Margaret was alive.

"It's cold today, I should not be surprised if we had some sleet."

"Cold, Miss Tippett, it's freezing! Snow is for the young and for the artist, but at my age, well, all I can think about is summer." Just saying the word made him see a meadow full of buttercups and wild parsley.

"Yes," Selina answered a little absently, for it hardly seemed possible that June would ever come again and— had she seen Ruby wiping a fork upon the inside of her dirty apron or was it imagination? Oh, dear, how careless the girls were getting nowadays, but if she spoke to them they started muttering about some factory. "I hope you were not too badly shaken last night?"

"To think that I should be able to live to stand the terrible noise."

"Have you tried ear plugs? They do say they give relief."

"But if anything should happen," Horatio objected happily, for Selina seemed to be in one of her rare conversational moods, "I think I should like to be aware of it."

"Isn't it better to trust to Fate?" It was astonishing to find the old clinging with such tenacity to life. What could poor Mr. Rashleigh get out of the days, she wondered; wouldn't it be glorious to pass suddenly to a legitimate, eternal rest? Angelina did not believe in heaven any more; that was very brave of her, of course, but terribly comfortless. "We have a nice piece of mutton today," she said solicitously, "be sure you get a slice." She stepped aside quickly to allow a woman to pass, who, as she expected, went up to Mrs. Spenser's table.

"It's a snorter, that word," Adelaide said, looking up from her crossword puzzle, "and how are you, Alice, after all this time?" Her sister-in-law had already acquired, she decided, the provincial look of the "cheap day-return" shopper.

"Oh, Adelaide," Alice fumbled with her coat and draped it over her chair so that a sleeve, of course, trailed on to the ground. Her hands trembled as she piled her parcels up on a vacant chair. "It's terrible."

"Well, Alice, I told you, you wouldn't like the country, not with your tendency to rheumatism. Why don't you move home to your flat? If we have a direct hit," she shrugged her shoulders, "they say we won't feel anything, and otherwise I just put wax in my ears and forget all about it. Do you know, I slept right through the alert last night?" She sat back, the pencil still in her hand, with the newspaper covering the table. "I suppose you can't think of a crested sea bird with six letters? Puffins have no crests, and there are seven letters in penguin."

"No, Adelaide, do you know ..."

"Soup?" Ruby inquired, her pad swinging from her belt like a bunch of keys.

"Yes, two soups; I expect it's tinned but we must eat something, and afterwards—will you have mutton, dear, whilst we can get it or do you want a macaroni cheese?"

"I'd prefer a health salad if they still have them."

Ruby nodded and disappeared into the kitchen. "Up to now they have been very good about serving fresh food, but gradually I suppose we shall have to get used to cans."

"Yes, but . . ." Alice leaned forward, and her old felt slipped almost to the back of her head. She might have put on something decent for the trip, Mrs. Spenser thought; once you let go, it was overalls and dressing gown in no time. "Really, Alice, you can't like those dismal fields, and I miss our little solitaire parties of a Friday, I do really; why ever don't you come back to town?"

"Listen, dear, I am trying to tell you something awful...."

"Don't say that your evacuees have measles; you know how very susceptible I am to *any* infection!"

"I'm trying to tell you," Alice shouted, almost in tears, "that I've just been machine-gunned!"

"*What*, dear?"

"Machine-gunned. In the train. It doesn't seem natural."

"Nonsense. Danger is the spice of life, and we won't give that man the satisfaction of thinking that we mind his antics."

"I know you were born to be a general's wife, dear, but I cannot think that being machine-gunned is an antic. I don't mind telling you, now that it is over, I was frankly nervous."

"Of course, I didn't say that it was pleasant, but what exactly happened?"

"Well, I woke up this morning with a queer feeling. First of all my alarm didn't go off, or rather it did; it woke me up at midnight and I forgot to set it again so I had a tearing rush to get to the station in time...."

"Alarm clocks are like the Government, always unreliable; they will explode at the wrong moment. If only we had been sensible in 1933 ... and even Thomas was worried ... there would be no Luftwaffe now peppering us with holes."

"Perhaps, but I thought something must be wrong when the nine-five went off exactly to the minute, because you know how late the trains are nowadays. I had a beautiful corner seat and I had just taken out my library book when the old man opposite began to snort. Adelaide, he was eighty if he was a day and he had whooping cough."

"How truly awful!"

"Yes, dear, I jumped up, grabbed my bag, and forced my way along the corridor, but by that time every compartment was crowded. At last I did find a seat beside a very old lady. She seemed to want to speak to me, and these days we must be democratic. Poor thing, her sailor grandson had just come on leave and had gone to the bookstall for a paper. Whilst he was there the train started."

"It doesn't sound a very auspicious beginning to your trip."

"No, and it jolted so much that I couldn't read, but fortunately I had my knitting."

"To quote a platitude, the modern woman's opium."

"Oh, Adelaide, no, it's not quite that," Alice gave a little horrified giggle, "but we stopped suddenly in front of a little wood. Have you ever thought how dreary one of those, I think they call them coppices, looks in autumn when everything is damp but there is still a tattered leaf or two clinging to the trees?"

"No, Alice, I always took a strong line about the countryside, particularly in October. It is a month only to be endured in England by the fireside."

"I sat there, thinking of Nature and of how it dies and is reborn with the bluebells and I remembered Mr. Chamberlain and how we prayed for peace. Why do you suppose that with all of us praying so hard, the war broke out as it did?"

"Because if people make guns it is human nature to want to use them."

"If only machines never had been invented! What we ought to do is to get together round the Peace Table and agree to give up machines, all of us, altogether."

"Nonsense! Somebody would invent a new lot next day. What is wrong with us is that we pigeonholed our foreign information. Thomas had a friend, you know, who went on a very dangerous expedition, and when he came back what do you think he found? All his reports in an official's drawer, never even opened."

"There must have been some mistake."

"Oh, no, there wasn't. They just knew he was telling them the truth and they didn't want to read it. He went off to the States, saying he was sorry that he had been such an idiot for twenty years. He warned us, ages ago, there would be a war."

"It was Mr. Chamberlain's heart," Alice protested conscientiously, "he was just too great a man to think about bombs."

"Then the proper place for him was in a bird sanctuary. After all, I value my life if you don't value yours.

And a thousand planes at this moment would be worth all the good thoughts in the world. But tell me, what happened about your machine gun, did you actually see it?"

"No. We went on sitting and sitting and I heard a very funny noise, just between us and the little wood. A man in our compartment went and put his head outside the corridor window. Then he came back and said, 'Do you hear that noise?' and I said, 'Oh, yes, it must be a threshing machine.'

You know it was a kind of popping sound. He looked at us and asked, 'Do you know anything about threshing machines?' and I said, 'No, 'and then he sighed and said, 'Do you mind if I smoke my pipe?' I said, 'Please do,' and then I dropped a stitch and it took me quite a while to pick it up again."

"And all that time you were just sitting still?"

"Well, dear, what else was there to do? Besides, I was so busy picking up the stitch. I do want to get it finished for Hyacinth's birthday. It is rather a nice shade." Alice delved into the knitting bag. "Do you think she will look well in rust?" She was always conscious of her sister-in-law's appearance, and though she despised concentration upon such worldly things there were wild moments when she hoped that her daughter might grow up into the same neat smartness. "You're always telling me not to be afraid of colour, but isn't this a shade too bright?"

"I'm sure Hyacinth will look charming in it," whatever the child wore it would make no difference, she had a permanently red face and a worried expression that did not match either her rural cheeks or inappropriate name, "but, go on, do tell me, what happened next?"

"After a time the train began to move again, ever so slowly, and we came to a station. The man with the pipe went into the corridor and said, 'Jerry got the signaller all right; look, they're taking him away,' but all I could see was a crowd."

"How dreadful!"

"Then the guard came along and told us, 'Got 'im in the 'and, they did, but it don't amount to much,' and my old lady fussed and asked if there was a ladies' waiting room at King's Cross and did I think her grandson would have to wait long for a train?"

"What a morning!"

"Yes, it really has made me feel quite funny. It is so—well—what you wouldn't expect. Taking the nine-five and being shot at, it's so unreal, and I think unnatural things are very unwholesome. Yet I used to feel the Germans were far more moral than the French."

"Oh, Alice, the danger of preconceived ideas! How often did I tell you not to associate the word 'discipline' with morality until you had found out what the Germans meant by it."

"Perhaps I was wrong, Adelaide," Alice agreed, doubtfully, "but we are suffering from too much freedom. Don't you think we are?" she pleaded eagerly with her eyes fixed on Adelaide's tricolour ribbon.

"The only discipline in the world that is *safe*," Mrs. Spenser pronounced, "comes from liberty. Why do you mind it so much?" It was useless arguing with Alice, whose thirst for submission was such that she enjoyed the war unconsciously because of the restrictions it imposed.

"I never have felt that we should be free to follow our own whims," Alice said, crumbling her roll, "but to finish the story, we arrived two hours late. And then, my dear, there was the poor old lady, looking so forlorn, standing on the platform beside her grandson's kit bag and naval gas mask. Of course, she couldn't have been a fifth columnist, but you know what people are like nowadays and I can't describe how they stared at her. I got her a porter eventually and told him to take her to the waiting room. Do you think the grandson would turn up?"

Ruby banged down two plates of pudding with even more vehemence than usual. Several of the shopgirls were already buttoning their coats. Horatio continued to sip his coffee very slowly, for even an empty Warming Pan was livelier than his own room. He wished he were not so deaf; had he caught the phrase "machine-gunned" in the conversation at the adjoining table? And what had happened now? Even he could hear the shouts. "Oh, how wonderful, Miss Hawkins; where *did* you discover him, oh, isn't he sweet?"

"Angelina!" Miss Tippett rose from her desk with her eyes fixed incredulously on her partner's arms.

At first only two scarlet gloves and the tip of a beret were visible, then Angelina set her burden carefully on the floor and stood up, smiling at her audience. Beside her sat a plaster bulldog, almost life size, with a piratical scowl painted on his black muzzle.

"Don't scold me," she appealed to the room, "wouldn't he be lovely as a stand for bulletins? And I do think these days symbols are important."

"Wherever are you going to put it?" Selina glanced helplessly from corner to corner; it was so like Angelina to spend money on a thing like that when they did not know where the rent was coming from. Oh, why were some people born with a sense of responsibility and others utterly, completely, and finally without it?

"Well, he's too large for the mantelpiece"—Angelina looked lovingly at her partner's desk—"you don't think, Selina, if we moved the ledgers?"

"I am sure he would resent so obscure a position."

"What about standing him in the fireplace?" Mrs. Spenser suggested, watching the Tippett's embarrassment with delight. "Where did you find him?"

Angelina swept off the beret that was worn only as a concession to the weather and ran her hand over the short, white hair that made a felt cap of her head. "In a salvage sale, opposite the Food Office. I can't keep a dog, I know, in the raids, but it's so cheerless without one. I was afraid at first that you might be tempted to call him Winnie, but then I thought, no, here is an emblem of the whole of us, so gentle, so determined ..."

"... and so stubborn."

Angelina glanced up suspiciously, but Mrs. Spenser appeared to be perfectly serious. "Stubborn! Oh, I see what you mean, we don't leave go, whatever happens. I should have thought that a better word was resolution. He must have a name, though. I shall call him Beowulf."

"How gallant, Miss Hawkins, but I'm sure he is a gallant dog." Angelina glared at Horatio, whom she loathed. Plaster is such bad taste, his mind was saying. "I bought him," she retorted, "not as a symbol of gallantry but of common sense."

An ugly woman, Horatio thought, and how she bullied her conscientious little partner, but at his age it was essential to keep upon friendly terms with everyone. "Ah, but you must not grudge us poor artists the luxury of dreaming about happier, courtlier days."

"I am sure Beowulf's monster wasn't courtly," she sniffed, bending down to lug the plaster object into the fireplace. An old fool like that would not know his history nor that Beowulf, unlike Drake, could be accepted by the proletariat. Had he not fought the dragon (merely a symbol no doubt for Viking dictatorship) to save the whole people? "You are right, Mrs. Spenser, the fireplace is just as good as a kennel." They all giggled at her little joke. "You know, I envy, I positively envy, that ribbon in your hat to make a collar for him."

Adelaide started forward, in mock haste. "Come along, Alice, I see it is time we moved." She patted the head in passing, "Good-bye, Beowulf, guard us well." Poor dear Miss Hawkins, how much happier she would be running a herbal garden with a terrier at her heels, yet how much more alive she was, though in a funny, childish way, than either Alice or the prim old Tippett! The preposterous bulldog that should have been simply vulgar really gave the bleak, dingy room an air of gaiety. He matched the feeding bowls, the "dog meals sixpence," and the faded views of country cottages to be let that still decorated the shelf over the counter.

Selina walked over to the window and looked at the cakes. She supposed that they would have to restrict them one to each customer like the other places in the district. But it would almost break her heart. Life ought to be generous, she felt, wildly generous. That notice on the wall, "Careless Talk Costs Lives," always reminded her of a morning in the last war when she had stood in line for hours to get new ration books. How bad-tempered Miss Humphries had been when she had got back late for lunch; the poor old lady had even hinted that Selina had spent the morning with Angelina, of whom she was so jealous. There were days when peace seemed the quick half-dreams she had if she woke up too soon and dropped off again for a few moments, and war was Time in all its ponderous duration. Yes, in spite of bombs, she would always see war as a queue and a yellow form with blank lines that had to be filled up with the stub of a broken pencil. People must live, but sometimes, waiting in line, she wondered why. She hoped that this wasn't what the Vicar called "questioning God's purpose," but she really was puzzled. A remote hand of destiny hovered overhead, something that even the Government was unable to understand; and as a result, cakes were cut, they were down to thirty-seven lunches instead of a hundred and seventy, and the fewer meals they served, the more people seemed to eat. Perhaps she would feel better once the afternoon post had arrived. Oh, dear, what was the cause of the war and why had Angelina bought that appalling dog? It cheapened, really it did, the whole atmosphere; and how shrewd of her to bring it back at just that moment! She could not reproach her partner in front of both customers and staff.

"Excuse me, madam!" Selina looked up at Ruby, who was waiting by her desk. She was fingering a crumpled overall, one that was kept, normally, only for washing up.

"I see, madam, you're wondering why I've got this on? It's to save my black. You never really get the grease out of a dark skirt."

"No, I suppose not," Selina stared suspiciously at Ruby's Sunday clothes; they never came out on weekdays except for some ceremony, usually a funeral.

"If it's the same to you, madam, could I take my afternoon off today?"

"Why, certainly, if you can change with Cook." There was undying feud between the staff, kept in check by another of Selina's rules: never interfere in quarrels and never take sides.

"Considering the circumstances, Cook is quite willing." Ruby began to sniff. "You see, it's mee poor friend Connie."

"I hope nothing has happened to her."

Tears began to roll down Ruby's cheeks, but instead of looking for her handkerchief she clutched her overall. "It was last night, madam. We had it awful bad our way. Do you know the Green Man at the corner of Station Road? It had two bombs on it. Parlour and all, there isn't a fragment left; it was just blown to debridge."

"Dear me, how tragic! I'm afraid I don't know the neighbourhood. And your friend? Was she . . . ah, at the Green Man?"

"Oh, madam, no!" Ruby was shocked and reproachful. "That's a public house and Connie never went to no pubs. She had the Stewdier opposite."

"The Studio?" Selina had a vision of a photographer's window full of big studies of grinning boys in uniform and those incredible postcards of little girls in white satin.

"Yes, madam, a Stewdier. Connie made the best jellied eels I ever tasted in mee life. Mee 'usband and I are partial to a bit of eel of a Saturday night. The last time I saw Connie," Ruby gulped and dragged out a handkerchief at last, "she told me that the war had upset the supply like and she didn't know 'ow she would keep going."

Dear me, Selina pondered, why does Ruby pronounce whole sentences correctly and why as suddenly does stewed eel become stewdier? How fascinating dialects would be if one had the time for them. Still, this was a moment for sympathy, not study.

"There's bricks from it," Ruby commented with mournful satisfaction, "right the other end of the road. They turned the buses off this morning, that was why I was late; but I could see the blue flag, that means they're digging for corpses. There won't be anything left to bury but I thought if I went and stood there in mee black, it would show my respect for Connie. So

I'll take mee afternoon today, if you don't mind."

"Of course, of course," Selina said hastily. Somehow the idea had all the paralyzing quality of the raids themselves. It had come out of the fibre of old, roistering, plague-ridden London. Perhaps she had overdone her refusal to listen to bomb stories; it might relieve the mind. What a difference there was, however, between the inexorable earthiness of Ruby and those timorous lady customers who flustered everybody, asking, "Will they come tonight?" "Standing in my black"— what a pity she could not rush to Angelina and tell her all about it. It made her partner's foolish purchase all the more annoying. Selina sighed, got up, locked the outside door, and hung up the sign, "Closed from two to three." There would be just time to check over the ledger before they began on teas. She opened the book, but the silent room made her jumpy. If only Angelina had not bought that dog! Her hand jerked (she really must get some mittens to keep her fingers warm; surely in wartime they would be permissible) and her pencil rolled onto the floor. As she stooped to pick it up she found herself staring into Beowulf's deep-set eyes. "Angelina," she shouted, "Angelina, you must come downstairs."

That placid, overfat plaster jowl was simply sneering at her. It was ridiculous to get as nervous as this; perhaps she had better go and make herself a cup of herb tea. Life—and she did not care whether the Vicar approved of it or not—life was simply unendurable.

5

IT WAS COLD. Ruby stamped her feet, waiting for the bus. She hoped that there was not going to be an alert. Whatever Ed might say, she was not going to spend another night in the shelter. It looked and smelled like a tomb. She would much rather lie under the kitchen table beside the fire than have her wrists knotted up with rheumatism before she was fifty. Yes, it felt as if it were going to snow and her bag pulled heavily at her arm. "Here's a nice bit of fish for you," old Tippett had said, trotting in just as she was slipping on her coat to leave, "and don't forget to take some of the stale bread for your cat." That was the advantage of the Warming Pan; they fed her well at midday and there were plenty of scraps but there was too much supervision, too much Selina following her around and saying, "We want to wash well underneath the shelves, don't we," or "Have you dusted the plates," when they would have to be wiped off, anyhow, before they could be used.

How much time had she spent, Ruby wondered, waiting for a bus? Once inside it there was warmth; you picked up bits of talk, noticed shop windows and the way buildings changed, but standing ... she could have lived her life twice over with the minutes and minutes that she had lost on street corners. Waiting for a bus, waiting for a bus; somebody ought to write a song about it, probably they had; what Timothy called a "swingy tune" just evaded her ears. The wind cut round her legs and she glanced back to see if there were many in the queue. All people at a bus stop were potential enemies. They might crowd in front of her, be among the "standing room for two only," and shove her back to wait an extra quarter of an hour. Today, however, she was early and the rush hour, or what had become, since the raids started, the "rush stampede," had not yet begun. If only the sirens did not go before she got home. She was a week behind with the wash, but when the kitchen was the only room where she was absolutely certain of the blackout, she could not clutter it up with damp sheets as long as they had to sleep there. She would soon forget what her bedroom was like; and Ed had done it up, new paper and all, only last summer.

The heaviest buildings had a fragile air as if children had cut them out of coloured paper and stuck them up in school with cardboard supports. If you poked a brick you were surprised that it did not crumple like a balloon. Even the bus seemed to have lost its authority; it came tearing down the empty road at the pace of a little car.

Ruby was the first to get on as it stopped. She pushed her way forward, for her favourite place was vacant, behind the driver. As she sat down, another woman in the next row looked up, greeted her, and came over to sit beside her in the neighbouring seat.

"Why, Mrs. Gates," Ruby said joyfully, "I 'aven't seen you for weeks! 'Ow are things your way, quiet?"

Mrs. Gates was as plump as Ruby was thin. She clasped her umbrella as if it were a steering wheel. The black fur circlet on her collar was thin and almost rubbed bare at the neckline.

"We didn't 'ave no bombs, but we 'ad some gunfires. It's a wonder we're any of us alive."

"It is!" Ruby spoke feelingly, groping for her coppers as the conductor came along. "Last week, it must 'ave been about seven. No, I mustn't tell stories, it was not much after six. Anyway, Ed had come in but I was sitting on the floor under the table, for the noise was something terrible, when I 'eard a commotion. I wondered what they were 'ip 'ip 'ooraying about and I says to mee 'usband, somebody's shouting at us. Go on, Mate, 'ee says, you're getting nervous. I'm not, I says, there's someone at the door. After a while 'ee gets up and opens it and there's a bobby. 'Pack up,' the bobby says, quickly, 'there's a bomb in the next garden. 'Urry and I'll take you down to the Centre.'"

Mrs. Gates swayed her umbrella to and fro. "A bomb, Mrs. Clark, 'ow awful!"

"Yes, mee 'usband says, but what about mee tea? I'm not moving till I've 'ad a bite to eat. Mee 'usband's not brave but 'ee's not nervous like, being in the Navy the last war."

"You didn't wait, did you?"

"Yes, but the bobby didn't. I'd got Ed a nice bit of cod, and 'ee 'ad that and two cups of tea. Come along, mee girl, 'ee says then, we'd better 'op it, but we didn't go up to the Centre, we went to Middleton's shelter at the top of the road."

"And did the bomb explode?"

"No, we was lucky. They moved it the next day. Maybe it was the rain; it poured all night, for I kept waking up and 'earing it, though they do say water make century bombs worse."

"Centuries?"

"Yes, them fire bombs." They were both nearly jolted from their seats as the bus pulled up suddenly. "Got a new driver on the route today. Suppose they took the young ones for the Army?"

"They don't care what they do to you, these days. Seems as if we none of us 'ad any rights. I've 'ad a bit of trouble meeself since I saw you last." Mrs. Gates leaned back luxuriously, visibly happy to have found an audience on so long a trip.

"Oh, dear, nothing bad, I 'ope." Ruby, having got her own story over, wedged her bag at the side and settled down to listen. She liked to have a bit of gossip to tell Ed over supper in the evening.

"I 'ad a slight operation like, at the 'ospital."

"And you was looking so well in the summer!" There it was, Ruby thought, what was to happen, happened; you could not dodge your fate. The pillars on the houses they were passing looked like the pipes you saw, piled up for road repairs, and the steps reminded her of soap. There was something spiritless about this terrace that had once been wealthy and now belonged to the empire of converted flats. They were without the conveniences of modern buildings and lacked the cheerful warmth of her own kitchen. She looked up at Mrs. Gates.

"The doctor said it was them oats."

"Oats!" Ruby was genuinely surprised. "I never 'eard before as they did anyone any 'arm."

"I 'ad pains." Her companion's voice was flat and final. "'Orrible pains. But you know what I'm like, I don't want to make no fuss nor push meeself forward. I'd rest and rest but it didn't seem to make no difference. My gentleman's away so I could put mee feet up too of an h'afternoon."

"Called up, is 'ee?"

"Same as; 'ee's in one of them Ministry places as 'as been h'evacuated. But resting didn't seem to 'elp so at last I went and saw mee doctor. 'Ee says to me, 'Why, Mrs. Gates, 'owever did you get yerself into such a state? 'Ow . . .'" the bus jolted again to another sudden stop and the handle of her umbrella flew forward against the window. ". . . 'e's a learner, 'e is. Can't ever 'ave got 'is licence."

"Debridge," said Ruby, rising to her feet and inspecting the roadway in front of them. "In a way, they clear it up quicker than you'd think."

"Well, mee doctor, 'ee's a nice young feller, no, you couldn't call 'im young exactly, 'ee's middle-aged like, 'ee says, 'I'll call up the 'ospital at once, Miss Gates. It's deep inside and it's pricked mee finger but I can't get at it.'"

"My dear, whatever was it?"

"I says, 'Well I don't want you to think I came to you for nothing, I thought I could cure meeself with care and suchlike, but it didn't seem no use.'"

"There's things you can't do for yerself."

"So up I went to the 'ospital and they put me under the h'eether, and let me tell you, Mrs. Clark, science is beautiful. Yes, in the old days they'd 'ave 'ad to 'ave cut me, but today they used a sort of tube, well, it was a magnet like, and they drew it out."

"Drew what out?"

"A tooth."

"A tooth, Mrs. Gates, but I didn't know you 'ad any. I thought you 'ad yours done when I had mine h'out?"

"Oh, it wasn't a tooth from me 'ead but a steel one from a comb. The doctor said, 'You must 'ave swallowed it with your oatmeal. I'd give it a miss for a bit,' 'ee says, 'and try something with more nourishment.' It's funny what you find in them oats."

"Sweepings," Ruby nodded portentously, "it's what 'appens to us working class. Not that I know h'anything of politics meeself," she added hastily, "it's what mee 'usband says."

" 'Ee's right, whatever 'appens we suffer."

Ruby was silent for a moment, for they were approaching the bridge; it was the bit of the journey that she enjoyed the most. She liked looking back over Chelsea, especially in spring when the lilacs were out, with here and there a flowering chestnut. Lambs, she would say, remembering her country childhood and egg hunts in the neighbour's meadow. She had never wanted to return to her village, people were too inquisitive, too credulous, always "nosing into one" as she complained to Ed, but she often wished that they lived nearer to a common. Then the river itself was a broad silver road leading to the sea. It gave her a feeling of safety and pride, her father having been a sailor. He had never been away long enough for her to forget him because he was usually on a coaster, but his visits home had been infrequent and marked by pennies to be spent unexpectedly in the village shop. She had always felt herself apart from the other families of ploughmen and bricklayers and it had made her restless; the same urge that had driven her father to sea had led her to throw up that good place at the Manor and try her luck in London. "Somehow," she said, pushing a little, for Mrs. Gates had taken advantage of the bus's swaying to grab more than her fair share of the seat, "I feel nothing can 'appen as long as the sea is round us." She looked out with satisfaction on a tug and a couple of coal-smeared barges floating on water that was the exact grey of their smoke.

"You're right, there," Mrs. Gates snorted, "not, mind you, that I'm against them foreigners but it stands to reason they can't be as 'andy as we are, never 'aving no sea to be on." A couple of gulls swooped from the parapet up into the misty sky. The next bridge, which they could just see through the diamond opening of the splinter netting, seemed almost silver.

"Ed says, 'ee don't think the German workers want war any more than we do; it's all That Man."

"For meeself," Mrs. Gates gripped her umbrella ominously, "there's only one thing to do with a Jerry and that's shoot 'im. Pity there couldn't be an h'earthquake to settle them once for all."

"Yet I worked for a German lady once and she was that quiet you wouldn't 'ave thought she was different from ourselves."

"Sly! That's what they are, and 'ow do you know what she was thinking? It's not my business, of course, but an English family's good enough for me. Still," Mrs. Gates continued affably, "times 'ave bin 'ard, I know; you can't pick and choose."

They had left the Thames and come to Battersea Park. It was empty but reassuring, for the trees stood, unlike the houses, with hardly a twig disarranged. There was even a glimpse of a circular flower bed, neatly dug up to wait for winter frosts.

"I see you're in black," Mrs. Gates went on. "I 'ope nothing's 'appened?"

"It's for Connie. She 'ad that shop at the corner of Station Road, where they got it so badly last night. Ed, 'ee's thoughtful like that, came all the way back to tell me. 'Ee didn't want me to see it, though of course they turned the traffic off, but I got out and walked along as far as the ropes. There's just a 'ole where the shop used to be; it's all stones and dust."

"They're not men, those Germans, they're fiends. Sometimes I think, though, we brought it on ourselves. There's no reverence in the young nowadays, they don't know what work means."

"Yes, the 'ussies, waggling about with their little caps and their perms. They don't get down to no scrubbing of floors like we 'ave to do. And what about our 'usbands? There'll be 'omes broken up in this war, Mrs. Gates, and it's these minxes as is responsible." Ruby had caught Ed's glance of admiration for a thing in khaki, with more money than manners, only the Saturday before; and Mrs. Gates nodded in solemn agreement.

"Now, Connie she was well off though I wouldn't say but what she's 'ad a 'ard life sometimes. Got into trouble and got out of it. She 'ad a good place with 'omely folk where she sat down to dinner; but her sister Vi was different, she worked at the kaff. That's where the girls met Alec. 'Ee's Connie's 'usband. It was Alec's friend who was going out with Vi. Posh boys they was, both of 'em, and Vi told 'em she was living at 'ome. Now, Vi loved her night out, but Connie was quiet like and when the boy found out that Vi was at the kaff, 'ee wouldn't 'ave no more to do with 'er. Called 'er awful names, 'ee did, that's what comes of telling stories. I couldn't tell a lie meeself, could you?"

"Sooner or later, we reap what we 'ave sown."

"Sometimes it's pretty late. I know a fishmonger who made 'is money in the last war but 'is misdeeds don't seem to have caught up with 'im. 'Ee's simply using 'is experience all over again."

"We must leave h'everything to Providence, and believe me," Mrs. Gates looked intently at her companion, "we shall not be disappointed in our trust."

"I 'ope not," Ruby said hastily, she had no wish to get into an argument, with poor Connie so much on her mind. "Well, Alec, 'ee married Connie and 'ee was a good 'usband to her, I will say that for 'im. Six or seven years ago the boiler h'exploded and it scalded 'er face, she 'ad a great scar down the side. But Alec was a fine man and 'ee stuck to 'er. Of course," and Ruby almost licked her lips, "she was a wonderful cook. I never tasted such eel pies."

The air began to fill with the smell of wet dust and burnt brick that was peculiar to a badly bombed district. It was a new smell for London, unlike either the musty odour of the plague pits or the charcoal rawness of a fire. This had a touch of explosive about it; subterranean gases seemed to have driven the ordinary, human atmosphere away. The houses looked shaky and desolate as if (and it was what all their occupants were thinking) they could not understand why the foundations still held. People were standing on chairs and ladders to tack wood or bits of canvas over the broken, empty windows.

"Connie never wanted to go out afterwards; I suppose she minded that scar."

"She had newsa-senior, I expect," Mrs. Gates pronounced the words slowly and carefully, "same as the soldiers."

"I keep thinking about Alec. 'Ee went back to the Navy in the spring. I 'ope somebody'll let 'im know. Think if 'ee came back 'ome and just saw the 'ole!"

"They'll give 'im bad news quick enough," Mrs. Gates sniffed. " 'Ere's your stop coming. It's bin a real pleasure seeing you h'after all this time. Drop in, if you come my way, and 'ave a cup of tea."

"Thank you, Mrs. Gates, that's very kind of you." Ruby picked up her bag and gripped the next seat as they lurched. "I 'ope you 'ave a quiet night and no warnings." She had to hurry, for there were few passengers and the conductor waited impatiently for her to get off. There was still a crowd by the ropes, sightseers mostly, staring at the ruins. The street was ankle deep in glass; it lay over road and pavement, in sheets, in broad jagged splinters and heaps of brittle crumbs. An old man was making a halfhearted attempt to sweep it into the gutter. Further up there were more officials. A lamp post lay sprawled across the ground, and somebody had hung his cap upon the solitary survivor of a group of railings.

Ruby edged her way cautiously towards the ropes. A paving stone had cracked, but instead of splinters it had bubbled up like dough. She could not get Connie out of her mind. This was a street that she had walked up a hundred times on Saturdays; the crossing was awkward, but once in the shop you were warm and you always felt the better, somehow, for seeing Connie. Not that there was much gossip, "It's best to know nothing in my business" was Connie's favourite remark, but she would listen to your troubles and tell you about her own whilst keeping quiet about the other customers. It gave you a feeling of confidence. How impossible it was that she should be there, underneath all that masonry! Instead of past and present running into each other like the river, Ruby looked at an experience that wasn't Nature, that was almost, she groped for a word ... ghostlike ... and even that didn't describe it.

"Good afternoon. So you've come up too?" Ruby recognized the speaker as a neighbour who was also "partial to eels."

"It seemed the least I could do." She unfastened a coat button in spite of the cold to show her black.

"Her poor husband! He is at sea, isn't he?"

"Yes, it's a funny world. Fancy coming back to this."

"I thought our end had come last night. I put a blanket over my head and stood under the stairs. It makes you go all taut like."

"Yes, now I lie down. I keeps mee clothes on, all but mee shoes, but I've made a bed up, under the kitchen table. Not that I sleep much," Ruby added truthfully, "for if you do drop off for a second the all-clear wakes you up again. Still, you can stretch out and it's warm."

"It's hard to realize that she's gone." Onlookers kept straggling up to stare at the mound where the houses had been. Now and then an official ordered them to move on, angrily.

"Look at all the people, blacking their noses. You'd think they'd 'ave something to do!"

"Perhaps they're Connie's friends, like ourselves."

"Admitted. But there's no call for them to be noisy," Ruby glared at a small boy who was kicking the glass in the gutter, "they could stand quiet." The disorder made her feel murderous, and if that child didn't stop he'd cut his boots to pieces and how would his poor mother pay for another pair?

Men never seemed to grow up; it was like Ed, who would wear the heels of his socks right out before he thought of tossing them to her to be mended.

It began to grow dark. The squad on the rubbish cone worked without turning their heads, but it was like trying to move a hayrick with wooden pegs. Now and again the pile creaked until it seemed as if it would split and engulf everybody. Ruby grew colder and colder; she could not put her left hand in her pocket because of her bag; how lovely it would be if she were Selina, the owner of the Warming Pan, without a care in the world. The customers might be in the country now but they would come back. She knew Londoners. None of them would stand a country winter. Imagine now having to worry about the price of coal! Her merchant had advised her to buy more before it went up again, but where would she find the price of half a ton or even the space to store it? She undid three more buttons. She would stand for a moment, thinking of Connie, then she must hurry off and get Ed's meal. "No use to mope," he would say if she were late. "'Ow about a nice cup of tea?"

A distant clock struck five. It was almost blackout time. Some rubble shifted and two of the diggers jumped cautiously to the ground. Tears rolled down Ruby's cheeks as the details of her last visit crowded into her mind. Connie had been less buoyant than usual; she hadn't bothered to turn the scarred side of her face away from the customers, as she usually did. "I may 'ave to shut," she had said, popping the last pie on the tray into Ruby's basket, "I can't get no eels." She had stared across the street as if the ocean were the other side of it, as puzzled as a lost puppy. "Go on, h'armistice will be 'ere and you'll be dancing down the streets with us before you've 'ad time to turn round." It made all the difference to Ed's temper if he got the tea he liked, and Connie was probably working too hard now that she was alone. "It's Alec I worry about," she had answered, slamming the drawer of the cash register so that it sounded exactly like a tram, "'e's so fond of the place, and sometimes I wonder if the Government don't mean to close all us small people down."

Now Connie and the counter and the shop were all part of the fire-swept graveyard, this rubble that was neither khaki nor grey but a queer colour nobody had seen before, sweeping up to the ragged brick edge that marked the first shell of the still standing houses. A knot of blackout curtains flapped from a hole that had once been a window. Ruby sniffed and wiped her eyes; it was quiet now that the picks had stopped, all that she could hear was a newcomer's violent sobbing. "I couldn't get no fish so I went to my sister's for the night. I wanted to match the teapot lid, the one that got smashed, and my sister said, 'It isn't right for you to be wandering round in all that blackout. You stay with me.'"

The woman, she was in brown with a veil round her hat, was staring at the pit in front of her. "Mee 'ome," she wept, and her sobs were small explosions in the silence, "mee 'ome, the boiler, the new blankets ... and h'everything. 'Ow shall I ever tell Alec?"

"Connie!" Ruby scolded in a shocked, reproachful voice, "you're 'ere, you're not missing and I'm standing around in the cold in mee black for you. Now don't you go getting yourself all fussed up and upset, we'll go to my place and have a good cup of tea. It won't do you no good to 'ang around looking at them stones; come along," she grabbed her by the arm, "and stop snivelling."

6

ANGELINA FLUNG HER beret onto the hand-woven quilt. They
had forgotten the curtains again. The war was a manifestation
of governmental incompetence, but as a citizen she would co-
operate with the blackout for it involved the masses as well
as herself. There was "neither rhyme nor reason," however,
she quoted firmly, in darkening the room during the day.
Just because she had forgotten to tie back the extra hangings,
Ruby had left them shut. They were more trouble to fix in the
evening but she wanted light, the whole world wanted light; if
people were wise they would hoard every moment of it, as the
silly bankers hoarded gold.

The window looked out over chimney pots to a plane tree
and a square of grey sky. Oh dear, Angelina thought as she
twisted the cord round the hook, there is going to be trouble
with Selina. The old dear simply has no imagination. Can you
believe it, Ella, she had said only yesterday at the meeting, my

partner never stops working and she'll listen to a hard luck story when I should bundle the miscreants out of doors, but she simply does not know what the word "vision" means. I cannot make her grasp the first elements of proletarian economy. "Liquidate her," Ella always joked, but you could not do that with the Tippett. Selina was classless; it was just that you could not make her see anything that was not, literally, in front of her nose. "Beowulf is a symbol for us, colleague" ("comrade" simply didn't suit Selina), but no, all the answer she would ever get would be "I'm afraid that plaster dog of yours will pick up a lot of dust."

It would soon be time for their early cup of tea, the very nicest moment of the day, Angelina felt, after the dull routine of the morning was over and before they settled to the evening's task. She looked up at the engagement list hanging over her chest of drawers, but there was nothing down until Saturday. She had always been what the French called "an amateur of meetings." It gave her such an illusion of travel to hurry off, sometimes before supper, to a hall in some unheard-of suburb of London; you had little adventures, it was most instructive, and occasionally you made new friends. There was that nice schoolmistress whom Selina disliked so much, merely because the poor woman would drop in for tea whenever she was in their neighbourhood, and the extraordinary Czech, whose name they could never pronounce. It added such richness to life, making so many contacts, hearing and learning so many things even if occasionally something went wrong, like the night that odious lecturer had insisted upon coming back with her and they had had, literally, to turn him out at three o'clock in the morning.

"Come in!" That must be Selina with the tea. She would

not say a syllable about being annoyed, but simply create a grey, fluffy atmosphere of rigid disapproval. Perhaps it would be better to say something at once to make it burst? Only this was such a pleasant time, and what harm was there in putting Beowulf in the fireplace downstairs? It wasn't as if he were alive and she wanted money for his food.

Selina pushed open the door slowly, trying to balance her tray. Now why couldn't her partner have opened it? Tea stains looked so ugly on a white cloth, and it was difficult, without spilling something, to turn the handle. "I've saved you a piece of jam tart," she said, poking at the small table that was littered with pencils, phrase books, and a scarf. "If you could make room, Angelina," she added patiently, steadying the two cups and saucers with their thin, blue dragons, which she always washed herself.

"Thanks, dear." Angelina swept the oddments up and dumped them, roughly, on the bed. The walls were the only tidy spaces in the room; and then Selina sat down, involuntarily, exactly opposite the poster that she disliked. A group of girls in summer dresses marched down its paper road, under an arch of Russian letters, waving flags. What a pity it was that Angelina had given up Esperanto! It had been a trial, of course, when she had insisted upon writing out the menus in that language, and she had brought that dreadful professor back from the Congress who had wanted them to put him up for the night; but though eccentric, it had been safe. Was it not a lesson to grumblers? A small evil may be removed and a greater one take its place. Every day now she expected to meet a detective measuring the picture, and to watch her colleague being hauled off to the police station, in that scarlet jumper that looked exactly like a railway flag, screaming things too, that must spell internment for the duration. I should be innocent, Selina reflected, but I should never, never, never survive the disgrace. This was no moment, however, to reopen their perennial quarrel.

"Did they straighten matters out at the Food Office? What are they going to allow us?"

"Everything's O.K." Angelina said briskly, "except the processed eggs. They say we are not entitled to them."

"But, Angelina, that's ridiculous. Did you explain to them that half our business is in the off-the-premises cakes? This powder is horrible, but if we are not allowed to buy new laid eggs any more, what are we going to do?"

"They have no forms suitable for our case."

"But, dear . . ."

"It's your own fault, partner, for being honest. You never have used anything but farm eggs. I have told you over and over again that honesty and private enterprise are incompatible."

"Don't be ridiculous," Selina said angrily, "whether it is public or private has nothing whatever to do with it. We always have bought direct from the farms since we started. Suddenly we are told that sales are forbidden, and I have no quarrel if it is *really* in the country's interest. But the shop up the road has an allowance; they told me so this morning. And, my dear, they didn't have to tell me, I could smell the stuff. But they are just as private as we are. Why shouldn't we have our ration too?"

"Because, dear, they have never used anything else but egg powder, and they have a record of their consumption during the past five years. It was stupid of you not to go in for all the counterfeits you could. I always told you so."

"It was not foolish to supply our customers or any human being with decent food." Angelina, she knew, was simply being tiresome. "It is my belief that we owe this war to changes in our national diet. Don't you tell me that our beef-and-beer grandfathers would have gone off to Munich with an umbrella!" Selina bit savagely into a second rock cake. Currants, she reflected, would be most difficult next season.

"It is just because you will not understand" (poor darling, how little Selina realized that only her partner's loyalty might stand between her and the lamp post at the end of the war) "the officials expect private traders to be dishonest. Still, I did what I could for you and there was a new, most charming girl at the Food Office. She went into the matter thoroughly. You see, there is no form printed that meets the case. Teashops have always used powder, and I suppose it occurred to no one in the Government that you had your special farm affiliations. The girl suggested that you write out the facts in triplicate and send it to the Board of Trade, and another, also in triplicate, to the Ministry of Food."

"But that will take time, and what about our cakes for Saturday?"

"They thought we might get an answer in six months." Angelina could not resist a slight tone of triumph; Beowulf's reception still rankled.

"Six months! It means we shall have to go out of business."

"Yes, dear." Angelina sipped her tea contentedly.

"But is there nothing we can do?" If they once shut down it would mean the end of everything, and whatever would they do about poor old Timothy?

"Legally, we are finished. But don't worry, Selina, I haven't got your inhibitions. I came out of that office, I must confess, in a state of extreme anger. So this is how the Government treats the little man, I was saying to myself, when I saw Beowulf in the shop window. He is going to bring us luck, you know, though we must not be superstitious." Giving up her little rituals had been Angelina's greatest sacrifice to her new faith. "Well, as I was saying, I felt depressed and annoyed and there was this bulldog looking ever so forlorn in the middle of a lot of battered tables, and I thought, you darling, I am going to give you a home...."

"Was he... terribly expensive?" Though if they had to close did it matter if they owed three hundred pounds or three?

"No, dear, not at all as it turned out. I went in, and in spite of the shop smelling musty the owner seemed a very pleasant man. I told him what had happened at the Food Office and we got talking about capitalism and the war...."

"Angelina! I do wish you would be careful. How do you know that he was not a plain-clothesman? You could get arrested under, what is that new statute, 18b?"

"That man a bobby!" Angelina snorted. "Anything but. He said, 'Now if you really are taking that dog and your partner is interested in egg powder, I've got a nice little lot here just come from salvage. I'll tell you where I got it. Remember that warehouse that went up the other night? Well, these tins were in the cellar and there isn't a mark on them. Like to have a look?' I inspected them, Selina, and I bought the lot. Fortunately, I had the money on me for the gas and the fishmonger. It was fairly cheap and we've got a year's supply at least."

"But is it legal?"

"Probably not. I didn't stop to inquire. I paid him in

pound notes, and he is sending it along tomorrow. Between ourselves, I think it was because he was glad to get rid of the bulldog. It looked odd in his window and, of course, he did not understand the symbolism as we do."

"I hope it is all right," Selina said doubtfully. "I wonder if we ought to put a notice on the cakes."

"What about?"

"Why, saying they are made with powder."

"Don't be ridiculous; nobody expects to buy cakes made with eggs these days."

"Honesty is the best policy," and Selina shook her head, "trickery does no good to man or beast."

"Honesty!" Angelina grunted. "And we have a plutocratic Government. Wait till after the war when we build up the 'new world.'"

"You don't think, dear, that it would be better for us if we learn how to use the old?"

"Selina!" Her partner gave a little scream. "Well, I'm not going to argue with you, there isn't time, but give me another cup of tea. I feel positively Robin Hood."

Exactly, her colleague thought, remembering the lounge at Bournemouth; that was all the trouble. People did not want to be shaken up by such stampeding vitality. While she would not wish to question God's purpose, it seemed a pity that no niche existed for her partner's talents. In Angelina you saw an elderly Englishman, smoking a pipe and strolling about a plantation. Civilization constricted her. And though this energy made her doubly dear because it was so unlike one's own placidity of life, it was disconcerting to strangers. "I can't help being worried"—perhaps, now she had accepted Beowulf, Angelina would be sympathetic—"we are a whole quarter overdue and I don't know where we are going to find the money."

Angelina wiped her lips after a final mouthful of jam tart. Cook certainly made beautiful pastry. Though how Selina could eat those heavy rock cakes she could not imagine; their very shape suggested stalactites. Her partner was dominated by her appetite, there was no other word for it. She, herself, never worried about food. "I don't care what I eat," was a favourite phrase of hers; it left one so free and unencumbered to face the future. Of course, a plump face like Selina's was never meant for leadership. Oddly enough, it reminded her of Beowulf, the Tippett so resembled a ladylike and gentle bulldog. "Courage, comrade," she saw herself in shorts, marching at the head of that column in the poster, "would it not be worth while to lose all this and gain New Britain?"

"Perhaps, dear, but the rent? I suppose even in New Britain we should have to meet our liabilities?"

"Oh, Selina, no! That's what I am always trying to explain to you. There would be no shops because we should own everything in common and the State would be responsible. We shouldn't have a worry in the world. Of course," Angelina added as an afterthought, wondering how they would organize an equitable supply of pastry, "we shouldn't have luxuries either."

"Do believe me," Selina continued patiently, pouring out two more cups of tea, "it isn't that I want to criticize your ideas; but if we shut the shop what is going to become of Cook and Timothy?"

"Couldn't we all do war work?"

"You know perfectly well, partner, that nobody would employ Timothy. He can hardly lift a broom, let alone a shell. Cook is fifty and Ruby has a husband to look after. And we, ourselves, are trying to feed the public at a very difficult time. Poor old Mr. Rashleigh, for example, how would he get his dinner?"

"Horatio is a man that has never been productive in his life. If he has got to be kept alive, and I sometimes question the necessity, let him go to an old men's home." "Well, it may be that in days to come your prophecy will be realized, though I am sure I hope I never live to see it, for I like running the Warming Pan and I can't think of anything to be ashamed about. But what worries me now, more than the raids, is how am I going to pay the rent with all our customers going to the country? It's getting worse every day."

"The owners are probably extremely thankful that we are here to look after the place." Poor Selina, her colleague thought, how she let a bourgeois environment dominate her! If the war only cleared away that horrible standard of "and I found a perfectly lovely chintz for my bedroom, dear," it would have one good deed to its credit. Down with homes, Angelina wanted to cry; why do we waste life in houses? All she had ever wanted was to be free and have interesting work. Everything would have been so different if she had been a man. People would not have resented then the surge of vitality that infuriated them in petticoats. *New*, that was a word that meant what heaven, she supposed, signified to most women. Oh, let anything come, anything that would lift her above the level of this grey, this teashop world. She could not help feeling exhilarated when the guns began, though she tried to remember the babies in the Underground, the mean warrens about greater London. She picked up the shopping bag that she had tossed onto the floor and began to go through a roll of receipts tucked into a pocket of it.

"If everybody leaves London," Selina said, collecting the teacups, "perhaps they will declare a moratorium?" Crockery was another item. The price was going up by leaps and bounds, and there seemed no ending to the pieces that Ruby could chip. She fitted the milk jug cautiously behind the plates; they could have bought a whole set, she was sure, for what her partner had paid for that wretched dog.

"You will never get anywhere by worrying."

"I know, dear, but I can't stop thinking; and when I think, I worry. I am going now to arrange about sandwiches. If you don't mind, I'd rather picnic in the shelter, because hearing that siren just as we are sitting down to supper gives me indigestion. I shall collect Rashleigh, because if anything did happen I should never be able to get him down those stairs, and Cook can fill the thermos with soup. After all, as long as the guns are firing it is very difficult to sleep."

Was it dampness or was it the camp bed? Selina rubbed her neck as she got up, it seemed to be permanently stiff and she must remember to take her liniment down with her. It seemed monstrous that they should all be suffering so much. War… it was like an endless succession of rainy days in a small country place on a brief summer holiday. Oh, dear, every winter brought her a year nearer that date (she had watched it come to so many) when the hustle of the tearoom would be too fatiguing to be borne; and she had dreamed, not of escaping it, no, there was a moment when evasion was impossible, but of pushing it just a little further away. If I had my life over again, she thought, staring at the empty, crackling twigs of the plane trees, I should like to be a housekeeper in one of those funny little City houses. What fun it could be to sit in a high attic with a gable, overlooking the crowded streets, at one not with London only but with the inner kernel of it, with those early moments when Chelsea gardens were a day's ride away. She imagined the pavement in the June light, a little fainter really than apricot, the men gone, the offices silent and herself painting (for if she were born into the situation that she wanted, she would also have the skill)... think of the history recorded in a solitary cornice! How often she had wanted to say to her companions, this is not dust, this is not smoke or cloud, it is a rainbow floating over battlements. Above all, she wanted to wait in the summer dusk and know that though it was holiday-time she did not have to go away and sit beside a bath chair on some promenade listening to Miss Humphries. London was unhealthy, Miss Humphries had always complained, but what was the using of living if you became a great, rank vegetable without any interests?

It was stupid to dream, her aunt had always reproved her for it, but tonight age haunted her. Poor Mr. Rashleigh, how sad it must be to feel sureness go, the skill of his hand. Worse than if he had never been a painter. What must he think of Beowulf? That dog... but she must try to be tolerant, it gave Angelina so much pleasure. "You will come down to the shelter, won't you, dear, before the guns begin? I know you'll laugh at me, but I have a feeling that it is going to be bad tonight. It makes me nervous to know that you are upstairs."

They could hear the shop door constantly open and close, as Selina went out with the tray; the girls from neighbouring offices were coming in for early tea before the stampede home.

7

MR. BURLAP WALKED straight over to the window. "Bricks and mortar, Miss Wilkins," it was his inevitable greeting but the new secretary was getting used to it, "bricks and mortar; ah, if I had my life to live over again I'd farm." He looked down at the square that was full of plane trees and a half-dug shelter trench. "If we had not drifted away from Nature we should never have had this horrible war. You would never find bird-watchers raking up the skies with those miserable aeroplanes." A silver barrage balloon floated above the black, desolate branches. "It's going to be a dreadful night," he said, wrinkling up his nose, "I hope I shall get home." His mother worried so when he was late and he simply could not afford to ask for sick leave at present. Everything was upset and the raids made him feel—it was useless pretending that they didn't—that life was not worth living.

"It must be a terrible journey, Mr. Burlap," Rose Wilkins

said respectfully, "especially now the days are so dark."

"Yes, it means feeling my way to the coach stop in the morning, and crawling along the lane in pitch blackness at night. But we have the stars, Miss Rosy Wings, we have the stars. You must not think that I blame your ancestors for the bombers. Peter Wilkins did his flying in imagination, that is its proper place."

"Excuse me, Mr. Burlap, but we never had a Peter in our family. My great-grandfather's name was Alfred, I looked it up."

"Dear, dear, I perceive that you have never adventured into the byways of our literature. Winged beings drew Mr. Wilkins, but his name was Peter, to an island full of marvels. A penny dreadful, Miss Rosy Wings, but a penny dreadful with a difference."

Rose had often changed employers since she had first gone out to business aged sixteen, but none of them had resembled her present chief. Some had shouted at her, some had been thoughtful, but they had all used an English she could understand. She did not mind Burlap's laughing at her, men liked to work their moods off on their secretaries, but his indifference was baffling. He was easygoing about lunch and his dictation was superb, but privately she had christened him "the Loon."

"I can still count five leaves." Burlap stared out of the pane that was neatly crossed with strips of paper; autumn was, he decided, a less disturbing time than spring. "But come, we must get on our treadmill or the wheels will stop; we have a busy afternoon."

How like the Loon to notice the branches and not the

condition of the room! Rose sat down primly and rigidly. Burlap glanced at his newly won carpet to give himself courage. It was only then that he noticed an unfamiliar space. "But, Miss Rosy Wings, why, what ... *where* is your desk?"

"They fetched it away."

"What!"

"Four men collected it while we were both at lunch."

"Collected your desk?"

"Yes, Mr. Burlap, they loaded it onto a van in the courtyard, the one that has just driven away. I did not give the men anything as I did not know the procedure. Ought I to have given them a shilling?"

"Tell me, Miss Wilkins, I am worried, I have been worried, but am I to understand that ... unauthorized persons have entered this room where I am engaged, oh, in a very humble and insignificant manner, in guiding the destinies of a war racked country and have removed the tool with which you aid me in such labours?"

"Yes, Mr. Burlap."

"And you did nothing about it, you did not protest, you did not summon the doorkeeper?"

"How could I, Mr. Burlap? They were within their rights. I am afraid you have forgotten that I only joined the staff three weeks ago."

"I am well aware of the fact. You still have not run folder X/Z 10342 to earth?"

"I am only entitled, sir, I mean Mr. Burlap, to a deal table."

"Of course, of course, I did remark that you were using an item of furniture to which you had no legal right, but this is wartime and how can we get on with that report, and without the report they can't have their machines, unless you have something to write on? Where is your table?"

"The foreman said that a Department in the country had been promoted, he wouldn't say where, it's hush-hush, but I think I know because the girl who sat at my table for lunch . . ."

"Yes, yes, Miss Wilkins, but *where* is your table?"

"The hush-hush groups are to have our desks and we are to have their tables, on Monday, I think."

"But this is Thursday."

"That's what I said, but the foreman shouted back that I could sit on the floor. I can't do that, Mr. Burlap, it's so heavy on the stockings."

Mr. Burlap looked out of the window to relieve his embarrassment. The barrage balloon was looking more of an aluminium sausage than ever. "The Government would never wish you to assume so undignified a position," he said severely, thinking of the hilarity the situation would provoke among the juniors. "We must use our initiative, improvise."

"I have sat on a packing case." There had been a glorious morning in one of Rose's first jobs when the manager had removed the office furniture in a van before his partner arrived.

"This isn't a question of a chair but a table." Burlap stared gloomily at the carpet that showed he was a seven-hundred-a-year man and saw with horror marks of muddy boots on the new surface. "What do you suggest we do?"

"I could bring my little bedside table with me tomorrow," Rose suggested, chewing her pencil, "that is, if they would let me take it on the bus. Auntie made me ever such a sweet little cloth to put over it, but it is plain deal underneath."

"I am afraid that would never do, Miss Rosy Wings; if anything were to happen it would not be on the Government records and we would be uninsured."

"If we have a direct hit," Rose said cheerfully, "there wouldn't be anything of us left to claim anything."

Such a different type from our regulars, Burlap thought, wishing that his previous secretary had not joined the A.T.S. "The proportion of direct hits per population, Miss Wilkins, is, as I am glad to say, infinitesimal. I have a friend in Statistics who tells me that at the present rate it will be several years before London is demolished. No, regulations are regulations and if in the flurry of opening this new wing we break them, you see the result! Without rules, Government cannot function nor can we bring the war to a successful end."

"I don't see how we are going to win it if we keep to them."

Burlap pretended not to hear. It reminded him of a painful altercation on the coach between a young pilot who should properly have been at school and a colleague. "Our first objective ought to be Minnie," the fellow had grinned, "I don't mind fighting but I do mind leaflets." It revealed a shocking state of part of the public mind.

"Well, I suppose we shall have to recast our afternoon. It is annoying because it will throw our schedule completely out of gear. I have an appointment at three," he glanced at the memos, "some fellow named Ferguson, you might find me his dossier. As soon as I have got rid of him I will go and call on Supply. Perhaps we can get the loan of a table for the morning."

"I believe that factory is waiting for your report, Mr. Burlap. Unless it's ready for the Committee tomorrow, production will be held up till next week."

"I could not regret it more, but if you have no table what are we to do?"

Nothing, Rose thought, nothing. If a private firm carried on in such a manner it would be bankrupt in a week; but public service was like a steam roller, it went in a straight line or it stopped. As her uncle said to her every evening, "Why should a Ministry be efficient, my girl? It hasn't anything to lose. Provided you get your salary, it is no concern of yours what happens. I can't stand a woman, and you know it, who pokes her head into politics."

"Mr. Hodgkins rang up in no end of a temper."

"I am afraid that is what is wrong with us as a nation, Miss Wilkins; few of our young men have learned the elements of procedure. Without regulations we have anarchy. I am sorry that our schedule is delayed, but we are not responsible. And once you have found that folder, I will give you permission to knit."

"Sometimes I'm glad my boy friend's in the Navy."

"Really, Miss Rosy Wings, I must ask you to keep your personal reminiscences until after office hours." Among war's disagreeable changes this enforced mixing with incompatible characters was the worst. He opened the top folder on his own desk and eyed it distastefully. "You know, Miss Wilkins, these papers should have been dealt with much lower down."

Rose opened the middle drawer of the filing cabinet and began to lift the contents out methodically. She wondered, as she had often wondered before, whether this treasure of flimsy carbons really helped the world to move. It was a dusty job and she wished that she had brought an overall to put over her clean blouse. Two pieces of cardboard stuck. She put her hand down and touched something soft. "Oo, Mr. Burlap, look! Biscuits!"

"Biscuits!"

"Yes, they've upset all over the back of the drawer. Are they samples, or shall I clean them up?"

Mr. Burlap walked over to look at the offending crumbs. They smelt of cheap fat and must. "Disgusting! Throw them away at once. But how could they have got into the file? I lock it personally every evening."

"I expect someone used the folder as a lunch plate." "Not in my Department."

"Perhaps it's a fifth columnist making signals?"

"I am afraid, Miss Wilkins, we must leave ideas like that to the pages of the popular press, where they belong. It is our duty, you know, as servants of a great community, to be cautious and sober in our statements. People look to us for guidance."

"But there were fifth columnists in France."

"Even a quisling could hardly use crumbs. No, Miss Rosy Wings, I fear that once upon a time you misdirected one of your sprites."

Miss Wilkins giggled. She was going to enjoy her supper, having the family listen to her for once. "And the Loon stood there," she would say, "with his nose puckered up, just not able to believe his eyes. The man doesn't even know what goes on in his own Department; but then, like all these Government fellows, he lives in a dream." "Call it a haze," Uncle would snort, "and we have to pay for it!" She shook the biscuits into a sheet of paper rescued from the wastepaper basket and sauntered off to the recess at the end of the corridor where they made tea, hung up their coats, and gossiped.

Mr. Burlap glanced up from his blotter, trying to formulate his plans for the afternoon. He wished his mother would understand that it was the war that made him late for dinner every evening. ("Perhaps when you have laid us all up with a bad dose of flu, you will catch the four-five.") The darker and more wintry the day the more necessary it was, as an example to the junior staff, not to leave a second before the appointed hour. With two changes and all the transport upset he could not help it if he missed the connection and got in at nine. It was a consolation to feel that the war was bringing his "blueprint age" much nearer, but he hoped that aerial traffic would be outlawed at the peace conference. He hated those youths who sprang into the skies overnight, disturbing the rooks and yelling at each other like footballers. Just then the telephone buzzed and the desk porter announced a visitor. "Colonel Ferguson? That's right, I was expecting him; send him up."

It was another of the volunteers, no doubt, who thought that they could gate-crash a Government Department just because the country was at war; one more symptom of the general slackness. Let them fight their way in, as he, Burlap, had done, from a grimy desk with a bus seat for a study. He could always recognize a colleague who had come from the same school mill as himself. There was an identity of purpose, a shade more precision in their reports. He could not disregard an introduction from Harris (people thought he would soon get his Department), but the interview, while friendly, might leave the applicant in the air. There was a knock, the messenger entered, and an old gentleman followed him with that air of assurance and good temper that Burlap so disliked, just the constituent, in fact, who prodded a Member to ask awkward questions in the House.

"Good afternoon, what news have you got of our good friend Mr. Harris? Do sit down, we still have chairs. Whilst I was in conference there seems to have been a slight misunderstanding about a desk, so this room is looking barer than usual. We've been flooded with new employees who will not learn procedure. There's a right way, I tell them, and a wrong; but they never listen."

Ferguson nodded; this time he felt that the interview was going to be definite. "I haven't seen Harris since I got back to London; he has been evacuated north."

"Yes," the lucky fellow, Burlap thought, I wish I were in his shoes, "he hates it, we hear, but it's wartime and we can't grumble too much, can we?" He gave his visitor one of those witty smiles that were "just pure Hollywood" as Miss Wilkins said ecstatically. "It would be disastrous if anything happened to the records."

"Of course. That is why I have come to see you. Harris thought with all the present dislocation you might have some work for me."

"It's rather late," Burlap said, chewing his pencil tip, "all the purely voluntary posts have been filled."

"I was living abroad, as I expect Harris told you. It took me some time to get back."

"What was it like on the Continent?"

"Oh, very interesting. Of course we knew that war was inevitable years ago, but people here would not listen."

It was just as he had surmised; Ferguson was another of those old-fashioned chatterers who were partly responsible for the present chaos. A type that had hated Chamberlain and talked irresponsibly about "liberty," as if it mattered that a frontier was changed. "What a tragedy this is," he said, "the Germans were such an orderly people." To Burlap, with his instinctive distrust of action, no more admirable virtue existed.

"They were really not very efficient, you know, except with their propaganda." It was curious how unwillingly the English gave up any tradition, but Ferguson himself had never found German organization particularly good. "Still, that's all over for the moment; what I want to do is help to the best of my ability."

"And what special qualifications do you possess?"

"I speak several European languages fairly fluently," Ferguson said with a faint touch of pride. It was fortunate that he had never allowed his mind to rust and that he had kept up his German translations.

"Languages!"

"Yes."

"Rather a drug on the market. I think, on the whole..." Burlap jotted a few words on the blotter, "it would be better not to mention them. I am not suggesting, mind you, that you are a fifth columnist, but you know how people talk? All this grumbling about the British climate is exaggerated. I have often watched birds in February, with only a light coat on."

Ferguson did not attempt to argue. He knew that sunlight suggested sin to many islanders, who seemed to confuse it with free love; and perhaps, he looked at the sallow face in front of him, a pale atmosphere suited some temperaments. "What about liaison work with the foreign troops? They must need someone, if only to teach the men English."

The very thing we want to avoid, Burlap reflected; it

was bad enough having the soldiers land, and essential to keep them from mixing with the population. These elderly volunteers gave way to a foolish kindness without a thought of the consequences. Besides, it was a bit suspicious, first living abroad and now wanting to work with a lot of Czechs and Poles. He wondered how well the old fool really knew Harris. "What is your experience? Have you a degree?"

Ferguson shook his head. "I have handled groups of men," he could not help a slight emphasis on the word, "since I was twenty, but I have no teacher's diploma."

"I'm afraid they're sticky about that now, you know."

"Yes, I suppose they are."

There really was no vacancy, but if there had been one, Burlap thought, he would choose his own man to fill it. Ferguson irritated him, for there was no knowing what was going on in the visitor's head. "I appreciate very much the offer of your service," he said with what was intended to be a warm smile, "but just at present I am afraid that your qualifications are impossibly high," it was better to flatter the fellow. "If you care to fill up this rather ... importunate ... form in triplicate and post it back at your leisure I'll advise you at once if anything turns up." He leaned back in his chair with a technique that had warned countless visitors that their interview was at an end.

"You mean ... you have no suggestion for me at present?"

"I'm afraid not."

"Then I must not take up more of your time." Ferguson reached for his hat.

"Oh, a delightful interlude, I assure you, in my dreary routine. Drop in for a chat sometime when this tiresome business is over. Where's your pass? I'm supposed to fill in the time you leave. Silly, isn't it?" He signed his initials with a flourish. "But rules are rules. The lift is at the end of the corridor; can you find your way downstairs?"

"Easily, thanks." Ferguson got up. "Goodbye, I'll tell Harris that I saw you."

The passage was full of girls chattering over cracked mugs of tea. Ordinarily he would have smiled at them, but now they seemed part of the unreality of the building. So the spirit— it came over him in a blinding flash—*could be conquered?* Perhaps when a world was doomed, each person, no matter how innocent, had to go through some personal destruction? This is the end and not a raid, Ferguson thought, jabbing the lift button impatiently. His Swiss friends had been right, he should never have come home.

8

"NOW, JOE," EVE SAID, stepping off the bus, "I know the name is funny and the place looks prehistoric, but the Tippett does have good cakes and lots of the gayer places ration you to one apiece."

"Anywhere you say, Eve, so long as there's food." It seemed a long time since lunch, Joe thought, and then there had not been much of it; between his father's liver and his mother's theories meals at home were always dull and cheerless. They never had those big steak-and-kidney puddings that he loved, with bits of bacon added and crusts soaked in gravy. They never had steak, with golden onions on top of it. He always said that he could count his age by his mother's experiments; she had stopped eating bread the week he had changed schools and had introduced nut cheese just after he had gone to business. If he had not been given his midday lunch at school he would have grown up too weedy ever to pass the medical. "Mother's

149

got a new diet," he giggled, "straight out of Food Facts. She sits by the fire all evening, nibbling a raw carrot."

"Don't!" Eve shivered. "It's worse than the time she fasted two days a week and sipped milk the rest of the time. Remember how you used to tell me about it at the office?" They grinned sympathetically at each other.

"Oh, she's crazy! Still," Joe added loyally, "she's good about everything else. She even cuts the football news out of the Sunday papers now to send on to me."

The wind tore up the narrow street, and Eve plunged her hands into her warm pockets. She really could not bother if this did pull her coat out of shape when it was so cold. It seemed strange to be here with Joe. She had not noticed him at the office any more than the furniture, the new linoleum at the entrance, or the shiny cover with a rent in it that always caught in the typewriter. It had been a complete surprise when he had turned up, half an hour before, on the pretext of thanking her for some cigarettes she had sent him, just as she was finishing her work. Time was hanging on his hands, she imagined; his father was in business and his school friends, like himself, were in the Army. He had looked round with an air of triumph, asked her how things were, and hung about, with his cap in his hand, until for sheer lack of knowing what to say to him she had suggested tea. He seemed so happy and self-confident as they strode along the pavement, a different boy from the one who had muddled up the envelopes and waited impatiently for Saturday afternoon and freedom.

"Here we are." Eve pushed through the Warming Pan door. It was so early that most of the tables were still empty, but on the far side of the room where a long narrow window had had to be permanently blacked out there was a light. This was the corner old Mr. Rashleigh preferred, and he was already in his place. Selina, for some reason, wasn't at her desk, and Mary, the kitchen maid, was taking orders instead of Ruby. There was a pleasant smell of baking, coffee, and warmth coming from the kitchen.

They sat down next to Horatio, to his mingled annoyance and delight. He loved to listen to people talking, but a nice girl like Eve ought not to gallop in, treating that boy with her (a brother, it was to be hoped) as if they were equals. "Two teas, Mary, scones and all the cakes you've got, please," Eve ordered. "My friend's just come on leave and he's hungry."

A visitor had left a bunch of asters from her garden. They were fading already into a smoky bonfire blue, though Selina had put them at once into her favourite pottery bowl. Autumn, Horatio thought, looking at them; they made him homesick for roads smelling of crisp leaves.

"How's food in the camp, Joe?" Eve inquired, getting up to hang her coat beside his, on the row of bright, varnished pegs.

"All right. You never know. The material's good, but you never know what the cooks will do to it." The chief thing was that rations were plentiful and there was none of the nagging home discussions about the harm meals did to the digestion. "My appetite kind of worries Mother; she's always telling me that I'll eat myself into my grave before I'm fifty. How does she know that I'm going to live to be fifty, anyhow, these days?"

When Joe grinned like that, with his round, blue eyes and rounder ploughboy cheeks, he looked exactly twelve and not a day older. "You can't expect your family at their age to keep pace with this world," Eve suggested. "Don't you find it hard to keep up with it yourself?"

"Guess I'm lucky," Joe said, pulling the cracked majolica ash tray over towards him. There were not many smokers here, by the look of it, but Eve was right, the cakes were wonderful and he bit a large piece out of his second scone. "I'm glad I'm living now, with everything changing and moving; it's such fun." If it had not been for the war he might have been stuck for life in that poky, dismal office. It made him shiver to remember it. He had a score to settle, not with the Germans, brutes though the Huns were, but with his headmaster. He could see Denham now, sitting regally at a desk and disposing of the future as if he, Joe, were just a bit of scrap. The walls had been lined with books and the blinds half drawn to shut out the summer day. The old tyrant hadn't even known his name, for Joe had watched him look it up in a drawer full of cards. "So your son wants to leave us," he had said coldly, coming down like a roller on Joe's dream of being a mechanic. "He'll regret it all his life if he does," and he had elaborated to Joe's only too sympathetic father all the reasons against his son's entering the local works. "Why, Joe is not like some of them here," the headmaster had insisted, "he will be able to take the exam in his stride next July, and there is, as you are aware, eventually a … pension." He had paused before that word as if it were too sacred to be uttered. But the Civil Service had not got him. No, Joe had ended that idea by failing his papers deliberately, but then his father had been so angry that he had sent him into the City within the week, just because he travelled up daily in the train with a man who wanted an office boy.

"Do you know," Joe noticed that Eve's plate was empty and he pushed the cakes across to her, "we had a talk at our camp the other night about New Guinea. A chap showed us pictures of the tribes and of the big idols they set up in their villages. They had the oldest, India-rubber faces streaked with paint, and people used to put skulls in front of them. They were so queer they gave me a nightmare afterwards; I thought one was chasing after me. The head was awfully familiar, and suddenly I remembered who it was." Joe swallowed another mouthful slowly; it tasted as if there really was some butter in it and he grinned. "It was my headmaster! I got a boot at my bed for making such a noise, but I lay and laughed till the tears came into my eyes. The same small eyes and a big stripe instead of lips. Before this war, each summer, we were taken up to him like skulls."

"You hated the office, didn't you?" Eve said. He had been a misfit from the moment he had come into the room, a big, burly boy who could not move without knocking something over. It was a comment on civilization, she reflected, that it had taken a war to settle him into his right place.

"Well, who wouldn't? It was just a live grave."

Eve offered him the final cake. She could not explain that to her the office was a haven, a place where she could grow, the first freedom that she had ever known. Rural life was delightful if you enjoyed growing peas and feeding chickens as her sisters did; but from the time that she could remember, she, herself, had liked cities. She loved the lamps coming out at dusk in peacetime, the sky that hung above the shops as if it were an orchid hung between blocks of buried masonry. It was less lonely here in a single room than in the crowded farm house with her sisters moving backwards and forwards with apples and knitting and chicken food, chattering and grumbling, "It's so selfish of you, Eve, to read when we want to talk." Joe was a kind boy but he was like her family; there were things in life that he would never understand.

Mary collected the cups with a great clatter from a table that two customers had just left. She wished she could persuade Cook to come to the Underground with her. Old Tippett disapproved of the least bit of fun. They had games in the big shelter and you could meet nice friends, like the boy at Miss Eve's table who was stuffing himself with muffins. Cook was stupidly afraid of the extra walk in the blackout, but it was not so difficult as she complained, if you had a torch.

"There are lots of opportunities now," Joe continued eagerly. "One fellow who had been an apprentice told me that we were learning more in a month than he had in a year. Things are moving so fast; why, they are flying speeds as routine that we thought were impossible, and it's come to stay. Do you know," he went on, in a sudden burst of confidence, "most of the time since I joined up I've been doing the things I really enjoy." He was only afraid that Fate might snatch him from machinery again, and he wanted to be sure that he would have oil on his hands and the rhythm of an engine in his ears as long as he lived. That and food. "Do you think," he asked, looking at the table, "they would let us have another plate of cake?"

Horatio looked up angrily at Mary as she passed his table with a second dish of gingerbread and scones. It was strictly against the regulations, but Miss Tippett, for some reason or another, was still upstairs. Didn't that boy know that there was a war on? The young seemed to have no sense of responsibility these days. Why did a girl like Eve waste her time with a lout who could not even talk to her; for nobody could call that muttering between mouthfuls conversation? People who spoke about living on memories were fools. Just to recall the Sunday evenings when he had moved among his pupils, speaking of art, was to know that he was just as capable of enjoyment today as he had been twenty years ago. It was opportunity—and money—that were lacking. What a calendar he could paint of Eve just as she was sitting now, her cheeks like berries in October's hedges; but he had nothing to offer her, he could not even, until Agatha wrote, invite her to a cup of tea. Yet she needed him to talk to her. "There are aspects of life," he would say, "that I hope, my dear, you will never know, but is it wise, do you think, to sit in a public place with that boy you brought in the other afternoon? Would your mother approve of him? Oh, I have nothing against the young fellow, and of course times have changed since I was young, but he was so obviously not ... not ... " what could he say, Eve only laughed if he used the word class, "... one of us. We should set our standards high, Eve, very high; and believe me, then we shall never disappoint ourselves." Horatio finished the last morsel of the solitary cake that he dared permit himself until at least some of the arrears he owed Miss Tippett had been settled; and then, leaning back in his chair, he scowled at Joe's neck.

Eve wondered desperately how to start another conversation. Boys naturally were enthusiastic about football, but it was hard to think of a phrase that would start Joe talking about it. They ought to have gone to a gayer place; the faded chintz cushions and the blackout curtains made the room seem dingier than it was. It was so quiet too that she felt every sentence must be overheard. She wanted to give Joe a good time, to make him feel the office still remembered him, but kind intentions alone could not break his impenetrable shyness. "You really like your camp," she said, realizing that it was the fourth time that she had asked the same silly question; and at that moment, looking round unconsciously for rescue, she found herself staring into the placid eyes of a huge plaster dog, whose wrinkled jaw precisely matched the chin of a woman sipping tea at the adjoining table. The resemblance was so striking that there was nothing to do but laugh.

"Now, Eve, what's up?"

Eve could only point. "Why breed bulldogs?" she whispered; and then Joe saw the resemblance too and grinned. "Boy! What a dog; wherever did they get it from?" he asked.

"I wonder! It's so unlike Tippett." The black muzzle was too smug and restful; for Selina acted, if she did not look, a lady with a past. "Perhaps some evacuated customer dumped it here? You couldn't take a thing like that on a train."

It added somehow, in spite of its vulgarity, to the atmosphere of the place. A few feet away the buses stopped on their way to and from the City, the Underground was beneath them, but here, as Angelina said, they had "a corner of an English garden flowering in our great Metropolis." You walked up to the Warming Pan if you wanted a recipe for quince marmalade or if Auntie had trapped a swarm of bees in her garden and had written for advice. Somebody was always there to embellish the information with lore and local anecdotes, just as if London were still a collection of villages along the Thames. There was a hand-drawn poster on the mantelpiece advertising a litter of terriers; gradually the numbers had been altered as the puppies had been sold, till now only a forlorn two, written up in red ink, remained. Yet the room was bleak; foreigners, Eve thought, would hurry away from its cheerlessness, but if it were destroyed, and she wondered if the spirit of a place survived a bomb, something draughty but kind would be broken. Perhaps there would be no more generations to potter in and out of gardens, plaiting straw hats and ready to murder each other over their delphiniums? How they had tormented her in childhood, calling her out to pick raspberries or shell peas; but once you had escaped, there was something proud and even perceptive about them. They respected your soul if they did not respect your leisure.

They sat in front of their empty plates, smoking. Eve hesitated to be the first to move, and Joe thought gloomily of the long ride home. In such a blackout there was not even the fun of watching his fellow passengers, and it was only too easy to miss the stop and to have to crawl a mile, feeling his way back by the walls. One or two customers left, cautiously lifting the curtain that kept the light from the street. "Oh, dear," Eve said suddenly, looking up at the clock, "do you think it will ever end?"

"What, the raids?" It was hard for a girl to have to go to work every morning, over rubble and broken glass, after a night in a shelter. "Look, Eve, why don't you join up? You could be out in the country with a swell group of girls. Don't let on that you've ever been in business, but make them train you as a driver." She would look grand at the wheel, he thought, instead of the old maid with no chin who came round with the van.

"No," Eve said, picking up her bag. "I didn't mean the raids, I meant the war." There were worse things than danger; there was this terrifying sense of having a cylinder full of fog clapped over one's face.

"The war?" Joe scratched his ear tip; the cold wind always made it itch. "Don't worry about that." It was strange how a girl's mind worked, but it must be that dingy office. He could not, now, see further than his brilliant present. "All we have to do is to be prepared. They couldn't invade us really, but they're so stupid they might try."

What is going to happen, Eve thought, staring at the broad, wind-burnt face in front of her; Joe doesn't want it to end. So many people were happy, really happy, now for the first time; and others, like herself, were suicidal. "I always wanted to see Paris," she said, then wished she had not spoken.

"England's good enough for me; you can't even get your own cigarettes the other side of the Channel, and a chap I know told me the food was terrible, all sauce and sawdust." He wondered superstitiously if it were good to talk about travel; sometimes a rumour flew around that they might be drafted overseas. "I might get sent to Egypt," he said, "but Africa wouldn't be ... "

"As bad as Europe," Eve finished the sentence for him.

"Well, you don't like foreigners, do you?" He was so sure that he never waited for her to reply. "Seriously, Eve, you ought to get out of London. This bombing—and, mind you, I don't blame you—is getting on your nerves."

"Oh, I'm all right. It's a splendid excuse to turn up late in the mornings. Instead of saying the bus was late, I just say I walked."

How hard it was for human beings to adjust to one another! The roots of war were always present in daily life, for it was not really crimes that upset people but their inability to enjoy the same pleasures. She wanted to travel and Joe wanted to take an engine to bits. Was there no way of persuading people to be tolerant, to let each other alone? Still, it was stupid to spoil what she hoped had been a successful afternoon by dragging in philosophy. War taught one to think deeply but to act and speak on the surface. "Anyhow, the only thing to do is live from day to day. It's Tuesday you go back, isn't it? I suppose you hate the idea."

Joe shook his head. "In some ways, you know, I'll be glad to get back." Camp life was more vivid. He did love Mother and Dad, but they seemed to talk only of ailments and old age; there was nothing in his own life that they really cared about at all. Home was stiff, he did not know what to say to them, it was all so different from the rough, warm, joking comradeship of his unit. Even Eve was aloof, though girls of course were difficult and he liked her calmness and her voice. "Well," he added, glancing up at the clock, "I suppose it's time to get cracking." It fussed his mother if he were out when the sirens went. "They have supper so early at home," he added, to excuse himself.

Eve tried to smooth things over. "Your mother gets tired, I expect, and likes her evenings by the fire. My aunt is just the same, the one I used to tell you about, she always eats at six."

"A nice place." Joe got into his overcoat and gave Beowulf a mock salute. Eve felt relieved as she stopped to pay the bill; she had been wondering all the time if they ought not to have gone to the West End. "They do their best with the cakes." It must have been the eleventh time that she had made the same remark. She pulled her scarf up to her ears and wished she were one of the people who always knew the right thing to say.

There was just enough light to see the pavement, but the sky was dark, it was a black violet with slits and tatters of a lighter colour visible between the chimney pots; a beautiful night for those who could forget the cold, but Eve looked up, missing the lamps. "Don't you wait in this wind," Joe said, as they turned the corner; "and next time," he added boldly, "you come out with me." By a stroke of good fortune the bus he took stopped just in front of them.

"Here's some cigarettes." Eve thrust a packet into his hand. "I'll write."

"Take my advice, get into the Army, and thanks awfully for the tea." He jumped onto the step. Everybody wanted to be home, and the conductor pushed the bell impatiently. Eve waved, but the splinter-net and the blackout over the windows hid the passengers as the bus rumbled off into the gathering darkness.

9

BEOWULF STOOD AS smugly in the recess that had once been a fireplace as if he had been its sentinel since the Warming Pan had opened. The painted muzzle might be lifelike at a distance, but to Horatio, sitting in the neighbouring corner, the jaws were those of a distorted monster, grinning at him from a cavern, symbol of the times and people rushing towards their own destruction. What an unfortunate day it had been, beginning with Dobbie's rudeness! He could have eaten, too, at least one dish of scones for his tea; these alerts surprisingly made one hungry. He shivered, for there was a draught, but he was not going upstairs yet, though Mary, he knew, wanted to chase him away. "I'm waiting for the post," he called, as she passed him, collecting the spoons and sorting them into a baize-lined wicker tray. "Don't bother about me."

"O.K., sir," Mary said, switching off all the lights except the one in the centre near the front door, "but do you think the postman will come? It's awfully late."

"I'm in no hurry." It was really worrying that Agatha had not written; a fussy, bad-tempered woman, Horatio thought, remembering how he had once caught her laughing at his sketches. It was petty, but the only time she had sent him even a Christmas card had been that year when his *England's Pride* had been in every stationer's window. He thought affectionately of the drawing, a clipper off Southampton Water with a hint of one of those sunsets he loved so much in the clouds behind the sails.

The door opened but it was not the postman, it was Eve. Horatio looked up in surprise, for a second door led to the staircase without the occupants of the house having to enter the shop. "I popped in to see if Miss Tippett was downstairs," she explained. "I wanted to ask her if she could spare me a cake occasionally to send to Joe."

"And who is Joe, if it is not presumptuous to ask?"

"Joe?" Eve's voice could not have been more indifferent. "He's the boy who used to work in our office."

"Times change, Miss Eve, times change. I venture to think not for the better. My sisters would never have allowed themselves to be seen in a public place with a complete stranger."

"Joe isn't a stranger, Mr. Rashleigh," Eve laughed. "We worked together at the same table for over a year." Old people were tiresome, they made everything so complicated; how could you make them understand casual office meetings and partings? Don't worry, she wanted to say, looking down at Horatio's white, thin hair. Joe isn't my boy friend, he doesn't care for anything except food and football. So direct a statement would shock the old fellow profoundly, and he looked so sad. "Did you have a very bad time last night?"

"I tried to conquer the torture of it all by making envelopes to save buying them, but who could work in such a fiendish din? At last there came a glorious silence, and I fairly sank into my armchair in which I rarely sit because I love my art too much, and Miss Tippett came in with a nice, hot cup of tea."

"Oh, that was where Selina was! I missed her from the shelter."

"It seemed to put new life into me, and the all-clear went immediately afterwards."

"I wish it would end." Eve wanted to go upstairs; the hours of her freedom were limited, but if she had to join up, and she supposed it was inevitable, she would rather scrub floors than go into a Ministry. The indecision of bureaucracy was unendurable. "Have you been out today, Mr. Rashleigh?" He was so forlorn that she felt guilty about leaving him.

"Yes, I had quite a walk this morning, although the northeast wind was bitter cold. I was dreaming—ah, now you are going to laugh—that I could hold one more exhibition of my charcoal drawings."

"I think you should," Eve said with vague hopefulness. She could see no future for Horatio, whatever happened. Even her sisters were against thatched cottages, and would be more likely to hang up a photograph of their spaniel than the best of Horatio's calendars. "Have you got enough for a show?"

Rashleigh shook his head. "Alas, with the scoundrel Nazis at the helm it is difficult to keep the Lamp of Art alight. Will you come and see my portfolio one Sunday, Miss Eve? And do me the honour of taking a cup of tea?"

"Oh, thanks, it would be a great pleasure sometime," Eve said cautiously; "at present we're so busy I even bring work home with me evenings." It was not strictly true, but she was more and more jealous of her hours alone; her doom was near, she felt it every moment of the business day. It was already a question of clearing up and shutting down; sooner or later the purely civilian trades would cease. Her sister liked the noisy army barracks where she was in training; it was, as she said enthusiastically, just like school. But Eve had no temperament for collective life. What a seesaw it all was! She was happy in peace and Joe in war; surely somebody could devise a means so that they could both enjoy their work without the continents being plunged into chaos. "Here's the post, Mr. Rashleigh," she said, as the door opened; it was a chance to escape. "I do hope we get a quiet night." The postman was in a hurry to get his round done before blackout; he slammed the mail on Selina's desk and left with a muttered "Afternoon" to Mary, who picked up the letters, sorted them onto a tray, and came over to Horatio. "One for you, sir, one for Cook, and the rest are for upstairs." She waited for him to move so that she could turn out the last light.

Horatio took the rather thick grey envelope; it was Agatha's writing. He had no excuse now for sitting in the tearoom any longer, though it was an economy of fuel and his joints creaked and he puffed wheezily directly he started up the steps. Extraordinary, he thought, extraordinary; my dear wife would never have believed that I could climb these three flights twice a day. He rested, of course, on each landing.

If he had to define to Eve the difference—the only difference—between her high spirits and his old age, Horatio thought, he would describe it as monotony. There were fewer breaks in the routine of unpleasant repetition. He paused opposite the door of the first-floor parlour that was now used as a storeroom. It was the sallow paint and the smell of soap and soda that became unendurable, at least to a temperament accustomed to the scent of grasses, a lacy parasol of leaves. Miss Tippett was a person of neither affluence nor taste or she would not sit behind a teashop desk; but she could have done something to this bleakness—repainted it, for example, some soft, attractive colour: green, a pale almond green with a grey carpet and a door that opened not on bins of sago but a bowl of roses. You could do a lot with a house as old as this, almost eighteenth century, if you only had the means. It is sad, my young friend, Rashleigh felt he ought to say to Eve the day that she had tea with him, to have the instinct for palaces and to be obliged to dwell in lodgings; but as a young man I had the whole of Nature for my kingdom. Yes, the sky was my ceiling with little, tumbling clouds making a medallion of nymphs above my head.

The chair was drawn up by the gas fire with a box of matches handy when Horatio panted his way at last into the attic. Mary had blacked out the window and left, as she did so often, a duster over the bed-rail. He hung up his coat carefully; perhaps tonight, if Miss Tippett were very pressing, he would consider the shelter. Then he settled down, pulled the rug over his knees, and opened Agatha's letter.

There was a cheque inside for the usual amount. Horatio slipped it carefully into his wallet: an old and shiny thing but solid, he thought, running his fingers over its dark leather. Nobody would know that a corner had come unsewn; but quality paid, it was seventeen years now since his wife had given it to him. He replaced it in his pocket and began to read the rather coarse handwriting.

"Dear Cousin Horatio, Here is your monthly allowance. As you know, this is a voluntary action on my part for you have no call on me or mine" (that was untrue), "and I feel I owe it to myself to discontinue these payments. The times are hard and I am obliged because of the war to retrench my expenses. So many sufferers need our help and my nephew, who you will remember joined up last November, is expecting an addition to his family." Of course the fellow would volunteer, his wife was always nagging at him. "I hope you have escaped our current perils. We had a bomb at the bottom of our street and in addition I have caught a severe cold, which has brought on my old enemy, bronchitis. Our shelter, unfortunately, is damp and though I have lodged complaints with the builders nothing has been done to remedy it. I trust my inability to continue your pocket money" (but it is all I have to live on, Rashleigh moaned) "will not cause you undue inconvenience. We must suffer our bit for the war. Your affectionate cousin" (no, no, Horatio almost screamed, she was never that), "Agatha."

It was impossible. Horatio dropped the letter onto the table and stared at the whorl of peonies that ran up the wallpaper. He must write to Agatha; hard as she was, surely she would be reasonable, for this was condemning a human being to death. People had no imagination. If they had they would project themselves into the lives of others; then there would be neither battle nor ugliness. His wife had always been so good to the woman; he could see Margaret now sitting behind the square, white teapot and saying, "Aggie's got another of her attacks. Do you think, dear, you could manage for lunch? Good, then I'll pop over and see what I can do." Slaved, she had, his dear Margaret, with never a word of thanks.

There had always been the barrier of money, whether they spoke of it or not. Agatha, and he scribbled her face, her mean little eyes on the edge of the envelope, had resented every gift he had made to his wife. "What about a rainy day?" she had cackled that last birthday when he had brought Margaret a gay little parasol with poppies all over it. He suspected he had heard her murmuring something about "old junk" when she went through the studio. We had a gracious life together, Horatio thought, and if Margaret's last illness had eaten up any funds they had had, he regretted nothing. "I regret nothing!" He said it aloud and fiercely to the wallpaper and the blacked-out window. He would be earning now, his hand was extraordinarily steady, if it were not for popular taste.

"I am glad my dear Margaret has been spared this." He wrote the sentence firmly under the sketch of Agatha. Perhaps Miss Johnson would write to him? He saw thin notepaper: "My dear Mr. Rashleigh, What a pleasant surprise to receive your letter in these troubled days. My mother used to speak of you and I have often wondered about you for somehow your address was mislaid. Do you remember the delightful water colour you once painted of our lupines? It is still here, in the same place, hanging over the piano. Now I know where you live, but to think that you are in London! Dear Mr. Rashleigh, if you will permit a stranger but I hope a friend to chide you, is it a place for a painter in wartime? They have evacuated a school to our village and artists are, they say, like children. Will you not accept the hospitality of our little home for the duration? We have no car, of course, but I have got out the pony cart, quite a museum piece, so with a wire I shall be at the station. You must get away from those horrible bombs."

What a triumph it would be! After a few days he would

write to Agatha, "Here in this peaceful seclusion where kind friends prevent even the news of war coming to my ears, I want to reply to your letter. It was a shock, I confess it was a shock, less because your allowance was insurance and not pocket money, than because of your uncousinly disregard of my welfare. In these difficult days the ties of relationship should be doubly knit, but it has been given to a patron of my art to look after me in the evening of my life. I am well, I am happy and painting as never before, with all my old enthusiasm and love of my drawing. And I have the sympathy of very dear ladies for having been so disparagingly treated. I will, therefore, say farewell as it will be unnecessary to continue this correspondence."

The tiny clock on the mantelpiece struck six. He ought to light the fire, but Horatio felt that he could not pull himself out of the chair. His legs were stiff, he huddled under the rug, shivering in the faint light of the bulb overhead. Perhaps Miss Johnson had gone away? She might never answer his letter, and then what would he do? First the calendar firm had refused a batch of drawings, then their works had been burnt out in the first days of September. Nobody wanted art any more. Only canvases centuries old, buried in museum cellars. He would die in this weather if they turned him out of the attic. Miss Tippett would help him if she could, but her partner, that frightful woman, grudged him even a pennyworth of care. Every moment was so precious. Every second brought him nearer to that blank, inexorable moment when ... but he could not name it, nightmare would triumph and he would not wake to see the sun shining in at his window. He looked miserably at the wedge of wallpaper beside the fireplace, and there in the crack a face was jeering at him; no, of course it was imagination; it was being angry, and he could hear his wife's voice: "Now, Horatio, you mustn't get upset, it makes you talk in your sleep!" The raids are less, he thought in surprise, than being reminded of that awful time when the neighbour's children had rolled him in the dust and sat on his head. The helpless fury, the wild terror of suffocation had remained more vivid (strange, how disagreeable things stuck in one's memory) than his first picture of any of his youthful triumphs. He had always loved trees and hated forests, for it was in the little wood behind the garden that his disgrace had happened.

Lawless, that was what the world was now, all the sweet virtues gone. He was glad that Margaret had been spared the war, though he missed her, he missed her horribly. She would have been full of practical ideas. "Don't fret so, Horatio," she would have said, "there's always the future." He must pull himself together and write to Agatha. Even if she halved the allowance, perhaps he could manage. Do you realize—he began to compose sentences—I am alone here, in the middle of craters? It was the injustice that made him boil. The news was enough to have brought on a heart attack with anyone less robust. There Agatha was, fat, with three meals a day and a home. It would have been reasonable to have asked her for more help to go away to the country. He was not through with his life, the sky was as blue, the sunlight as welcome, as ever. He tried to picture a sailing ship, as he did when the warning sounded, but tonight even that comfort failed him. There was no safety; the wallpaper flowers were like heads, grinning and leering, though he knew it was his fancy. He was shivering, and it was with fear; this was his home, and people said they were fighting for their homes. Perhaps he would tell Miss

Tippett when she came in, as she always did, to persuade him to go to the shelter? Selina might sympathize; or would her face change, would he see her think, well, if a lodger can't pay the rent why does he want to live? No, he could not tell her tonight, he would wait till the morning. In the morning he must write to Agatha....

Perhaps there would be no morning.

10

IT WAS A QUARTER to seven. The siren might sound at any moment, and then the wardens were particular about torches. However often she made the trip to Mr. Dobbie's shop, it was still a nightmare to Selina. Either she fell off the pavement or she bumped into the grating of the house next door. There was something morally reprehensible about the blackout, and in spite of the raids she could not crush out a feeling in her heart that "they" had decreed it merely to upset daily life as much as possible.

Selina began to bundle up her blankets into an old rug-strap. Her bed was stripped under a much-washed counterpane, and this gave the room an air of transience; it made it, she decided, rather like a warehouse. She had never had enough money to furnish it properly, with "nice pieces" such as the bureau that Mrs. Spenser had once shown her, with smooth drawers and a cedar scent. People did not realize the high cost of neatness.

Her almost obligatory uniform, the blouse and tweed coat and skirt, were far more expensive than the vague, elaborate clothes of many of her customers. The skirts would get shiny no matter how careful she was; she brushed them, wore the two suits alternate days, and had never been known to stain them, not even in the damson season, but they wore out with constant use; and so the curtains, which had really been faded before the war began, were never replaced and her cupboard could neither be shut nor opened in a hurry.

If she could have one really long night's sleep in her own bed, she would not feel so depressed, Selina thought. It was doubtful if Mr. Dobbie's basement, smelling of coffee and sacking, was really safer than the house; only she could not leave poor old Mr. Rashleigh alone in his attic, and there was no knowing how Cook and Mary would behave, left to their own devices. There were moments when she wished that they slept out, like Ruby. She pulled the strap tighter round her bed roll, and the worn leather came away in her hand.

Selina stood looking at her luggage, at the blankets and pillow sprawling over the carpet and the small, heavy suitcase with the documents and her other coat and skirt. She could not endure any more, she thought, there must be a limit to endurance, though there didn't seem to be. Her arms would not work, and she could not think. Cook went downstairs heavily; it was a signal that she was late. If she did not hurry, Angelina, who was, alas, so restless, would get that creaking deck chair. She ought to find a piece of cord (her mind outlined the actions, as if by listing them they were accomplished) and knot the two bits of strap together, but she was too tired; she sat down in her chair again and remembered, for no particular reason, a day when Miss 'Humphries had been particularly trying and one of the big black trunks had got mislaid at the station. She could see the palm tree now with the branch split in two behind the little wicker tea table and hear Miss Humphries storming at her, so loud that all the people in the lounge had stopped to listen: "Surely you know, Miss Tippett, that two and two make four? I thought you had counted the luggage at the station."

It had been on the tip of Selina's tongue to resign her position right away. She had heard a lady giggling, and everyone had stared at her. Why, it had been the moment, and it came back as if it were happening all over again, when she had first met Angelina. A figure had strode over from the desk, with such untidy hair, poor, dear Angelina, it was so characteristic of her, how much better she looked now that she had had it cropped, and had said, "Trunks, did I hear that you have lost a trunk? Those incompetent fools at the station did the same thing with my suitcase the other day, but the stationmaster ought to have been in the diplomatic service. I can't tell you how kind he was. Do let me ring him up for you—he found my things at once." Miss Humphries, who had an aversion to strangers that was almost eccentricity, had been so charmed that it had turned out afterwards to be the best holiday they had had for years.

I must be tolerant, Selina muttered, leaning over to roll up the covers again; if that wretched bulldog means so much to her, I must try not to let her see that I think it's vulgar. I wonder how much she really gave for it?

Still, they had got the processed eggs, Miss Tippett reflected, as she tried to thread a piece of too short string through the buckle of the broken strap.

There was an ominous silence in the street. How easy it would be to sleep, at once, in her chair. Somehow Selina shook herself awake and pulled on her woollen gloves. With all her belongings under her arms, she looked like a porter. I ought to have an armlet, she thought, catching sight of herself in the mirror. How grotesque in the twentieth century, she almost said aloud, shuffling up the staircase to tap at Horatio's door. "We are *all* going down to the shelter tonight, Mr. Rashleigh; I'll come back for you as soon as I've taken along the blankets."

Some obscure sound came from her boarder's room. The usual ritual of objection, she supposed, only half listening to it. "Now, Mr. Rashleigh, you must remember it is not ourselves we have to consider. I need you to help me with the girls. They turn that basement topsy-turvy without our supervision."

Dear, dear, how trying the old could be! Selina started downstairs, trying to keep her bundle from flicking each step and catching all the dust. The handle of her case cut into her fingers, but she could not make three separate journeys. How much longer could this go on, she wondered? Her neck was permanently stiff, and if she got much more rheumatic she would not be able to write up the ledger. Perhaps she was a fool to bother about Horatio and Cook. If the poor old gentleman wanted to die in his bed, it was really more sensible to leave him in peace; only then she would feel guilty all night, knowing that he was alone in that insecure attic. Nor was it really her affair if Cook had hysterics and screamed. Why did she go on dragging herself to the shelter, why didn't she stay on in her own room and sleep? Sleep, she thought, it was a silver word, a smoky silver. At the thought of it her eyes half closed; and then, of course, the makeshift handle of her roll slipped and a pillow began to bulge. She stopped under the faint blue light on the landing to repack and rest.

Nobody had noticed in peacetime how steep the staircase was. It must be a very old house. The shadowy walls stretched above her head like cliffs, and then, as she turned the corner for the final flight, she seemed to be staggering into a mine. One of these nights somebody would trip over a rug and fall to the bottom. She stopped suddenly at the thought of it, feeling her knees catch against an invisible rope.

Mary was still fumbling at the front door. "Must have been the raid, yesterday, madam, it seems to stick." She was in the new siren suit that had caused so much excitement in the kitchen, but the hood was too big and it had fallen back on her shoulders. She tugged the handle angrily and the door opened with a jerk. Selina dropped her bundle to switch off the light hastily, hoping no wardens were outside. "Timothy said this morning it must have shaken the frame."

"Oh, it will take years to put things in order again," Selina said, staring up into the dark sky. What wicked people those Germans were, always making wars. The headlines seemed continuous: the Somme, that nephew of Miss Humphries getting killed, victory, and now, in spite of all those Armistice Days (Miss Humphries had never missed being wheeled into the park for the Silence), it was happening a second time in an even more unpleasant way. I wonder what it is really all about, she thought; only it was a good thing not to have said this to Angelina! "Dear, dear," she managed to switch her torch on in spite of her thick gloves, "we live in difficult times."

"Cook says we should be ever so much safer in the Tube."

"I'm sure we couldn't be cosier or more secure than we are. It is very kind of Mr. Dobbie to let us come to his basement.

And it is much healthier than being underground with thousands of people."

Mary was unconvinced. She pulled her hood forward wistfully, looking like a gnome in a pantomime chorus. "Cook says they have games in the station and her sister met ever such a nice gentleman, he had a radio no bigger than a sandwich box. It was ever so gay." She slammed the front door shut and picked up the tea basket.

There was just enough light to see the railings round the area of the neighbouring house. Selina felt her torch slip gradually from the hand that was trying to hold both it and the strap. If her blankets came unrolled in the filth of the street she would never feel like using them again. She had to walk so unnaturally too, taking tiny, stiff steps like a penguin, partly because it was so difficult to see and partly because of the weight dragging at both shoulders. I know I shall get sciatica next, she thought, for the cold pierced her coat as if it were not wool but porous blotting paper.

It was strange how seldom she had been out at night. There had been a ban on darkness in her youth, and Miss Humphries, of course, had never stirred out after sunset. How frantically they had searched through timetables so as to be sure to arrive at Bournemouth in daylight! "My dear Miss Tippett, fancy suggesting the two forty-five when you know how prone I am to bronchitis!" The siren and that querulous voice had something in common. At the Warming Pan, life had been too full to encourage nocturnal excursions. Occasionally Angelina had dragged her to a theatre, but plays were either unpleasant or exaggeratedly romantic. And as for the cinema, she positively disliked it. It was associated in her mind with the more tiresome of Mary's moods, or with Cook's unending descriptive frenzies after her evening out. Yet this darkness, cold and difficult as it was, was strangely beautiful. The ugly block at the bottom of the road became a fortress—and had she seen archers scrambling up the turrets in the front beam that was not a swinging lantern but a small, electric torch, she would not even have been surprised.

"Don't wait for me, Mary," Selina said, "the sooner you get out of the cold the better." Another figure bumped into her, hurrying up the street, but it was as quiet and shadowy otherwise as if she were walking up a country lane. There was no light showing from any window. The houses stood in flutes of dark stone with no visible entrance. She tried to hurry, for she had a feeling that Mr. Rashleigh was going to be troublesome, but she had to set her suitcase down twice before she reached the door that Mary was holding open.

It was a relief to get into Mr. Dobbie's hall and to struggle down the twisting staircase to his basement. One end was blocked up with wooden boxes, but a dozen people had already arrived and were making up their beds as usual the length of the two walls. "So this is the twentieth century," Selina snorted, by way of greeting. Her rubber mattress with its red and green stripes looked incongruous on the concrete floor. Angelina considered herself an unofficial warden, and was already checking names and deck chairs by a pencilled list. "No, Cook, I shouldn't leave the thermos there, it will be in everybody's way; stand it in the corner, our 'refreshment room,' and are you sure, tonight, you have remembered to bring the biscuits?" She moved a chair rest, picked up a pillow, and came over to Selina, as if there had not been a shadow of disagreement between them. "Welcome to our Lido!" she shouted gaily, waving to someone on the stairs, and the room really was like a bathing pool that had got mixed up with a side show at a fair. There were grey rugs like horse blankets, pale pink quilts and striped sun-bathing pads. "I've hidden the barley sugar, dear," she whispered, "so be sure not to ask for it. You know what people are like, and I will not listen to them sucking it all the evening. It might be the saving of our lives if anything happened."

"We shouldn't be able to enjoy it, should we, if we were covered up with rubble?" Candy was a weakness of Selina's, and just the mention of it made her feel how good a stick would taste at that very moment. It was such a pity that her partner was narrow minded over what she called "nibbling between meals." Then she remembered the fruit drops in her bag; she would eat one going back. "I'll leave my things here and go and fetch Mr. Rashleigh; I won't be five minutes, and then I'll help you with the chairs."

"That tiresome old man!"

"I know, dear, but I can't sleep when he stays there, all alone."

"Oh, well, hurry then. The chalk is working beautifully; I'm marking numbers all along the floor."

Angelina had evolved a theory that a line should be drawn between each bed; but as there were too few for the room to be crowded, it seemed unnecessary. She was very happy, however, with her stick of chalk. It gave her the feeling that she was organizing the neighbours into a big, happy community, and she planned, but dared not suggest, a wall newspaper.

"I'm afraid, Mary, you neglected to sweep up this morning," Selina heard her partner saying, as she started up the stairs again; "greasy paper is not only unsightly but it attracts the flies. All of us," and Angelina flicked the checked duster reprovingly, "are helping to keep the shelter tidy, but Cleanliness is Essential." She folded a shawl and straightened a pillow whilst Mary looked on vaguely with her mind on her own affairs.

Outside, the road was ominously calm. Mr. Dobbie must be at the warden's post; he was a very comforting figure in his tin hat and blue uniform. Walking was easier without bundles, though Selina stumbled over one curbstone; but Mary was right, the door did stick, and she had to use all her force to open it. It would be unpleasant to be trapped inside, and she ventured to leave it ajar. As she entered, the long, familiar moan began that was taken up, second after second, by a dozen other sirens across London.

The Warming Pan, empty as it was, seemed full of rustlings and shadows. How strange, Selina thought, climbing the endless stairs; in a few seconds they might be blown to bits. Still, they said you felt nothing with a direct hit, and though she murmured the words, the meaning slipped away from her. A step creaked and she stopped, listening for footsteps. It was tiresome of Timothy, he always had a new story about looters. As she passed her own bedroom door she had an impulse to dash in and collect the trifles from the shelves; they seemed to reproach her for leaving them. What an irrational fancy to have, she reflected, but it showed how easy it was to become terrified by one's own imagination, whenever violence upset normal existence.

Horatio was sitting in his chair, staring at the wall. "Hurry up, Mr. Rashleigh, all the girls are waiting for you at Dobbie's and I can't manage them without your help. Why, you never put on your gas fire!" Selina looked round for his overcoat.

"You must be frozen!"

"Beggars can't be choosers, Miss Tippett!" Horatio made no attempt to lift the coat from his knees.

"As long as you paint your delightful landscapes"— she must humour the old man—"how can you speak of want?" There was a new sketch of a girl on the mantelpiece; she resembled Eve a little, sitting on a bank with a ribboned hat in her lap. "Is that another picture? We must take it down with us and show it to Mrs. Spenser." She tried to force his stiff arms into the sleeves.

"Oh, just a *petite* water colour nobody wants these days. I call it *June*." Flattered in spite of himself, Horatio let her draw his gloves on; it was the first time that he had seemed really helpless. His hands were blue and cold, and he made no attempt even to button up his collar. "If this goes on," Selina chattered, folding up his rug, "we shall have to take to sleeping bags. I wonder if you could manage to carry your pillow?" He seemed not to hear her, and she had to lead him to the door, though he stopped and picked up his little painting as they passed it.

Once Horatio's light was out, the corridor seemed endless. It was impossible to hurry him, though Selina thought grimly of the scramble they would have outside without a torch. They bumped down, a stair at a time, but though the rug was lighter than the suitcase, Rashleigh let his full weight drag on her arm, and she was afraid that they might both topple forward to the bottom. He did not speak, and she had a sense of the walls being alive, of shadows watching her, laughing at her, as if the thoughts of people whom she had never known, the original dwellers in the house, had been released from cracks and keyholes. It was unnatural, there were no other words to describe it, and she had never had so lost a feeling before except once when she had missed her way in a fog.

"It's not far," she said reassuringly as they stepped into the street. Was it imagination or had it really grown clearer? "Did I switch out the light?" she asked, and to make sure she flashed her torch inside the letter box. Even if she had left her money or keys upstairs she could never go again through that dark hall. She rattled the handle to make sure everything was locked. "Now, Mr. Rashleigh, slowly and steadily; are you on the pavement all right? Let's count our steps and we'll be at Dobbie's"—she had been going to say—"in a moment," but the guns started, like a pack of wolves, and the road itself vibrated under their feet.

"You know, I think this blackout is worse than the raid!" Selina felt for the railing and began to creep forward. They must look like two blind pilgrims in one of the grimmer mysteries.

The noise was tremendous. It was not like thunder, it was angrier. Planes seemed to be directly overhead as if the whir of a mosquito had been magnified many times. "Take my arm, Mr. Rashleigh, we must hurry!"

Swift movement, however, was impossible. Horatio merely upset her balance, and she wondered if she ought to jettison the rugs. There seemed to be nobody in the street at all when the flashes lit up the darkness. They lurched along as if they were on a rolling ship, and the cold wind started Mr. Rashleigh coughing.

Half the sky seemed to explode over their heads and crash. "It's all right"—she tried to be as gay as possible—"they say if you hear them it isn't so dangerous."

"Thank you, Miss Tippett, but I am going back." Horatio jerked his arm away and turned. Something whistled down a few yards along the road.

"You can't, Mr. Rashleigh, you can't!" Why, the obstinate old fool, he would never find the door; he couldn't get up those stairs alone, and duty or no duty she could not enter that house again tonight; no, not if it meant a lifetime of regret. "We are almost there, and then we can have a nice cup of tea."

"I prefer to hug my own hot-water bottle; we can only die once!" He started walking with amazing rapidity back towards the Warming Pan.

"You can't!" Selina shrieked, grabbing his shoulder quite roughly. "The door has stuck, and we've got to get into the shelter. That was shrapnel."

"It's the noise, the terrible noise...." Horatio put up his hand protestingly and at that moment Selina tripped over the fringe of the rug. She fell into the arms of a figure who stepped out of a doorway, saying, "Can I help?"

"Oh, Colonel Ferguson!" She recognized the voice.

"We are trying to get to Mr. Dobbie's basement." Ferguson took Horatio firmly by the arm. "Come along, it's not a healthy night for any of us to be abroad. Suppose you go ahead, Miss Tippett, to show us the way?" He tucked the bedding under his other arm.

The sky was a soft velvet that flashes turned into a gala of exploding candles. The guns had stopped momentarily but the planes seemed at chimney level and directly above them. People are dying every minute, Selina thought, but I can't realize it; nothing seems real. I don't even know whether I am frightened or not. The glow from a fire a long distance off lit up the doors, and she did not have her usual struggle with the keyhole. They led Horatio inside; he was muttering something but they could not catch the words.

"Oh, there you are," Angelina shouted; "I was beginning to get worried about you!" The sudden light in the basement was dazzling. Some people were knitting, others were sipping tea. Selina glanced at her watch; she had been gone only twenty minutes, and it had been like three hours. She sat down heavily in the first armchair and began to pull off her gloves. "You know, dear, I said there was going to be a bad raid tonight, but now it's come I don't know whether to be glad or sorry that I spoke of it."

"Madam always knows," Mary said gravely. "Why, she told Ruby the other morning, hurry up and fetch those apples, there's going to be a warning. And sure enough, there was."

"I didn't know you were a prophet, Miss Tippett, as well as a cook," one of the ladies said, putting down her cup.

"Oh, it's not prophecy," Selina said modestly, "it's just rheumatism; I feel it in my bones."

11

IT MIGHT BE BEARABLE, Eve thought, sipping her tea, if the atmosphere were less like a boarding school. The teachers enjoyed themselves, Angelina, old Miss Hill, and Dobbie the warden, but the pupils, civilians like herself, sat miserably along the wall, the victims of a vast, destructive bureaucracy that was the same in every land. It was impossible to realize what was happening. Angelina had compared raids to a film, but the screen was at least concrete; it was easier, she decided to her amazement, to accept a photographed storm as real than this concentrated bombing. It was the absurdity of it all, the dropping of balls upon the ninepin houses, that baffled understanding.

Even in the few weeks taboos had grown up; the people chattered incessantly as they came in about the events of the day as though this would prevent untoward happenings at night. Beds were arranged in the same order, less because of comfort than from fear that to alter the original sequence might mean a worse night. Thermos flasks marked a solemn pause: afterwards, whether you gossiped or not depended upon your neighbour. War was the triumph of bad organization, Eve decided; there was Joe, completely happy as he never could have been in peacetime, and here she was herself, her world broken, her future darkness and her present almost unendurable. "Now I know just what you need!" Miss Hill's voice, which was so much heavier than her small, bustling personality, rang out above the rest of the conversation. "Juniper oil; I took five drops myself this morning." She reached under her camp bed for a handbag.

"It's just nerves!" Her victim, who had the air of a rather pale mouse wrapped up in a grey shawl, leaned back wearily in her canvas deck chair. "I'm sure the noise must affect us subconsciously."

"Nonsense, dear, my grandfather used to say, what do you mean by subconscious?—we got along perfectly well without knowing it existed! But I knew you'd upset your digestion, drinking that tea at four o'clock yesterday morning."

"I seem to get so cold."

"Well, the juniper oil will put you right. It was a better England, when we gathered our own remedies and baked our own bread. And I wish I had lived a hundred years ago myself."

"I expect our ancestors had their troubles too."

"But they didn't have the radio. Directly the wireless started blurting out a lot of unnecessary news like a town crier bellowing about a mad dog, I knew something would happen. All this gossiping out loud, you could almost call it eavesdropping, is unnatural."

These wretched women, Eve thought; if old Hill says another word, I shall have to go back to my room. The zipper of her sleeping bag had caught in the fringe of her coat and she tried to focus her attention on disentangling the strands. She would much have preferred to stay upstairs in bed, but it upset the Tippett, and Selina was the only person in the room who was really kind to her. People talked about progress, but when you came down to happenings and not articles in the press, the same old Victorian life went on. They accepted the Warming Pan because it belonged to the kitchen, was domestic, but her own job was taboo. There was nothing people hated more than independence.

The guns came nearer. Occasionally there was a screech of brakes as an ambulance rounded the corner. "That's just a door banging," Angelina called, as an old lady, hearing the thump, struggled out of her bed.

"Well, what I say is, these shelter evenings encourage correspondence!" Eve's neighbour, the only other "business girl" in the room, looked up from the rose-pink linen note-paper case carefully arranged on her knee. She was sixty, the cashier at the stationer's up the road and came, not from the Warming Pan, but from her own attic somewhere else in the neighbourhood. Selina and Eve had christened her privately "Miss Empire," for she had nieces in New Zealand, a brother at the Cape; Muriel, "my colleague all the time I was at Jackson's," was in Montreal, and there was another friend in Vancouver. Lilian herself (her name was inevitably Lilian) had never left her London birthplace except to visit a married sister in Exeter, but she had exchanged her mind, Eve always pretended, for a post-office guide.

"Did you really look today for cards?" The Christmas mail was the axle around which the year revolved. It was less the fires and the German armies that Lilian feared than the disorganization of the posts; she was forever quoting precedents from 1917.

"Yes, dear, how kind of you to be interested in my spot of worry. I wanted to find an English hunting scene to remind my nieces of England's picturesque joys, and today, in town, I secured one. A calendar. It does look bright and jolly and typical of England's winter days, but it is difficult somehow to reconcile it with all this," and she looked round at the bundled-up forms on the mattresses and chairs. "I would have kept it to show you, but I thought in these times we never know what is going to happen." She giggled as though she had uttered a rather naughty word. "After all, I do feel that they will look after the mails if it gets really bad, rather than us citizens. So, somehow, I felt safer when I had popped it into the slot."

"Yes, that was wise, I think." It would be silly to remind her of the smashed pillar boxes and the burnt-out vans. Perhaps she felt that the use of the term "royal" made them invincible.

"In the last war, my sister's eldest boy, he was only two, got the Santa Claus I sent him only at Easter. I was always so vexed. He must have thought his old aunt crazy, sending him snow when he should have had a bunny."

"You cannot do more than post at the date they advise."

"No, dear, but somehow I always felt that I should have been more careful. After all, our festivals only come once a year. Has it ever struck you what a time we spend preparing for them, and then they are over in a flash? It's difficult to think about Christmas with those raiders overhead; still, the

British Lion is barring every door, and the more it is banged, the tighter it will hold."

"People are being extraordinary."

"Well, what I say is, it does not do to give way to things. I used to tell Muriel that, when she got so frightened over thunderstorms. I missed her very much at first, for if a person has lunch with you for ten years continuously the day seems upside down when she goes away; but now I am thankful she is in Montreal. We don't always realize at the time how often things happen for the best."

The basement vibrated with the shock of masonry falling in the near distance. It was as if they were lying at the bottom of a well with nothing overhead. All the heads stared up in unison, a grotesque sight, for what use were looks if the sky itself collapsed? There was a moment's silence, and then the knitting needles began again, though one or two, with furtive glances at their neighbours, helped themselves to barley sugar.

"If paper could speak, what a tale your card could tell when it gets to New Zealand!" The pillar box began to bob up and down in Eve's mind until it was an ark swimming on dark tropical seas. "I saw a film once, I remember, about a bank note. They ought to make one about your letter. I should begin with the mail"—she thought of the taxi roof that she had seen that morning on her way to work, just visible at the rim of a gigantic crater—"then there would be the docks, the ships being loaded in spite of the fires, the submarines in the Bay, at last, after the fear and the stars, sunlight on the other side of the world." Only nothing really would explain their experience; there would be a gulf between the bombed and the unraided.

"I don't know"—her neighbour began to sharpen a pencil—"if I do go to the pictures I like a real story; a good cry once in a while makes you fresher for your work."

Eve could think of no suitable reply. "Oh, I'm one with you in appreciating the spring weather," she heard above the clatter. "How glad we shall be to say goodbye to winter, though it has to come again in a year of months. I love the moment when the snowdrops bloom in our little yard, though this year everything will be on the tapis, methinks." And Mrs. Juniper Oil's niece (Eve did not know her name) settled back into her creaking chair, as if raids were the most normal thing in the world. "I do not think the outlook is too safe, just now, though Britain's hope for victory is great."

"Safe," Colonel Ferguson murmured to himself, looking up in amazement. Was it courage or was it simply stupidity? He caught Eve's eye, and both smiled. The barrage blew up in a gust of thunder, died almost away, and then bellowed again, until he thought of an illustration he had seen somewhere of men crouching in caves. Perhaps civilization was really unbearable, and in some rage of protest man had duplicated the conditions of the beginning of the world? It amused him to think that the distant thuddings of the mobile guns were the footsteps of mammoths.

Perhaps too much security was unendurable. Families said that they were afraid of war, yet they were unwilling to take one positive step to prevent it. Oh, they joined pacifist societies and smothered criticism, but they had never once looked the monster in the face. Colonel Ferguson shut his eyes, remembering a summer afternoon in the Wrights' garden, on his last brief visit to England before the war. "I know you two like exchanging reminiscences," Mrs. Wright had said, snipping off a faded delphinium head into her basket, "but if it had not been for those wretched trenches Frank wouldn't be a cripple with his rheumatism. What idiots you were! But it isn't going to happen again, you know, we'll see to that," and she had clipped off another lavender-coloured spike almost to ground level. "What about Germany?" Ferguson had inquired. "War, they think, is all that matters."

"Tush! Scare-mongering. It's the newspapers playing up atrocities, and I don't believe they happen. It would be a better thing for the world if the press were abolished." And the Parliament and laws, the Colonel had felt tempted to answer. "It is true," he had protested, "I met a boy in the mountains. On a track I had found by accident, the real smuggler's path. I thought the child, he couldn't have been more than seventeen, had had an accident. At first he was terrified, then when I could not answer his German he realized I was English and showed me his hands. They had been broken by rifle butts. The Nazis had left him for dead, and an old woman had helped him to cross the frontier. It was his turn yesterday, but it may be ours tomorrow."

"You have a kind heart and he took you in. I expect he was just a common criminal."

"Even so," Ferguson had wanted to reply, "you don't smash a boy's hands." It would have spoiled the afternoon for Frank, so he had answered simply, "No, it was true, I made inquiries." Now they were all learning about war the hard way, for the second time in one generation; yet sitting in this basement and looking at the diverse group in their rugs and siren suits, people still seemed unaware of what had happened. I know and I understand, he thought with great bitterness as another explosion shook the street; but it is all useless, people prefer stupidity. He felt in his pocket for his cigarette case, but caught sight of the notice Angelina had chalked up in large letters, "No Smoking During Alerts."

"Dear me," Selina sighed, "it is being noisy tonight! I must confess I find it trying night after night with no sleep."

"Do try some wax plugs, Miss Tippett, I'm sure they would help you." One of the many old ladies dived into a huge bag she held, full of goggles, ointment, and powder. There was a violent crash as she spoke, on a neighbouring roof.

"Patience, my children," Angelina shouted from the top of the stairs, "wait until you hear the eight o'clock news tomorrow," and she mimicked the announcer: "'There was slight enemy activity over London in the early hours of last evening.'" They all laughed, but several stirred uneasily in their chairs.

"I think it is better not to try to settle till the guns stop," Mrs. Juniper Oil intervened. "I go home directly the all-clear sounds, take a bath, and sleep on till eleven."

I can't do that with my ledgers and my stores, Selina thought, yawning. Horatio was staring at her in a very peculiar way, like a child she had once seen who had been frightened by a runaway horse. "Don't worry, Mr. Rashleigh," she called across to him, "five minutes more and we'll have some soup."

"Hush," he whispered, pointing to the staircase, "they're after us."

"Of course, they are after all of us." It was best to humour him. "But here in the shelter we are safe."

Rashleigh shivered violently and shook his head. He could

distinguish forms in the shadows, dancing and leaping. "Can't you see the flashes?" he muttered. "They've got to the stockades."

"Stockades? Whatever do you mean?"

"The Indians..." He broke from Selina's grasp, for she had crossed over to quiet him. "There, can't you see them?" He tried to crouch under the staircase. "Indians..." he yelled the word, but nobody heard him, for the walls lifted with a roar at that moment and split, and rushed towards each other in a cascade of noise, plaster, and crumbling bricks.

12

"ARE YOU HURT, madam?" Selina realized gradually that the shouts were meant for her. The darkness was worse than the staircase had been, and she found herself kneeling on a mattress, clasping an enormous pillow. "No!" The word sounded like a scratchy whisper, though she was yelling. "No, I don't think so." A memory came back of being forced to stand as a small child almost underneath a waterfall, and of fearing that it would choke her.

The guns had not stopped, but there were whistles everywhere. "Stay where you are, don't move and we'll have you out in no time!" With infinite relief, she recognized Dobbie's voice. Then the paralysis lifted. "Angelina!"—this time she really screamed—"Angelina, where are you, are you safe?"

"Yes, dear, but thanks to myself, not the nation. The cork has been blown out of Miss Hill's thermos and the soup has scalded her leg. If we had had deep shelters this would never have happened. I shall write to the *Times* about it!" Somebody kicked against a fallen chair and ... was he injured? ... Horatio was whimpering in a corner.

"There, that's better!" Ferguson, who had been thrown to the ground with an old lady wriggling in his arms, managed to disentangle himself and flash on his torch. Part of a wall had come down but the beams above the shelter had held, and though the occupants and their Lido of beds and chairs had been flung like a trampled ant heap onto the floor, there had been no serious damage. "We're all right, Dobbie," he shouted up, "we can manage if you're wanted elsewhere."

A fog of dust, smoke, and unknown smells enveloped the room. People coughed and laughed. Plaster fragments slithered from the walls to plop on the ground like hailstones. "If only I could find my bag," Lilian wailed. "It's got my ration book in it!" There was a great central silence, Selina noticed, in a multiplicity of little noises. The guns broke into an even more savage barking, and they could hear the buzzing of enemy planes. "I wish they would not remind me of a mosquito," Ferguson grumbled, shaking his overcoat.

"Has anybody got a torch? I've lost my bag and it's got my ration book."

"My dear, this thermos is all right. We can have some tea."

"Pull yourself together!" Angelina was slapping Cook's back violently. "What do you want to cry for? We're safe!"

The zipper had caught again, of course, and Eve tore at her bag to get out of it. Lilian's papers and a camp stool were all over her legs. It was like a Goya drawing, she thought, frantic black shapes in an underworld lit by one faint beam. Horatio was muttering between his sobs and somebody suddenly screamed. The sensation of having her legs tied up was definitely unpleasant, but the blanket gave at last and she scrambled to her feet, still holding a strip of it in her hand.

"Now then!" Dobbie came carefully down the staircase with his big, shaded torch. "The sooner you get to your cups of tea the better. These steps seem all right, but come up one at a time. We can't have old folks like yourselves sitting around in a draught."

Nobody moved. They were choked with dust, but there was a strange unwillingness to leave the remains of the shelter and go into the open street. "Come along, Miss Tippett!" The voice was stern. "You know where our Rest Centre is, so suppose you lead the way."

Oh, dear, Selina thought, I really can't endure any more darkness. I want to lie down and sleep. If she had to move there ought to be a flying carpet to transport her, or she should be able to shut her eyes and wish herself there. Mechanically she flung her blanket over her shoulders and picked up the smaller of her suitcases. The handle was gritty and she bumped into a dazed figure still kneeling on a mattress. No, I can't be first, she wanted to say, but at that moment a low, terrifying moan came from the corner: "They've got me, my head, save me..." then the words blended into a meaningless cry.

"Get them out of here as soon as you can," Dobbie ordered, hurrying towards Horatio. "And tell them we want a stretcher." Somebody else found another torch, and the procession, once it had begun to move, crawled up to the pavement. The door had been blown in, but workers had dragged it away.

Selina's first instinct was to rush towards the Warming Pan, but a complete wall of smoke as thick as a hill advanced towards her, and before she had time to think, Ferguson grasped her arm and hurried her round the corner. The side street had been untouched, and was not too dark, for there were several fires now in the neighbourhood; the flashes and flares reminded her ironically of bright moonlight. There ought to be another expression for such light, but she could not remember one; all she could do was to relate new terrors to old experience. "I wonder what happened to the house," she said, but Ferguson only walked along more quickly. "Oh, I expect it is all right. Do you know where the Rest Centre is? I don't."

"Keep that torch down!" somebody yelled in a very irritable voice. The shelter group had been dazed and motionless until as they began to use their limbs the hurry of flight possessed them. They streamed after Miss Tippett, shepherded by a warden, except for a few of the younger ones who dodged into the smoke at the heels of the rescue party. I wonder if it is like the Great Fire of London, Eve thought, as she tried to find the Warming Pan. It was and it wasn't, she decided. It was true that the dark shapes grouped themselves into the forms of some old canvas and the colours were less black and purple than a patina of oil, age, and dust. Yet there was a new element of violence that was beyond apprehension and rational emotion. It had scooped out, somehow, a part of her own being.

"Keep back, keep back," people shouted. Gradually the fog lifted and they could see flames. A bomb had hit the corner next to the restaurant, and as a result the Warming Pan was simply not there. The staircase that Eve had run up and down so many times had disappeared except for the bottom flight of steps. Her room was air. All that remained was a table, upright, with two plates on it and Beowulf standing quietly under the mantelpiece.

"I can't believe it," Eve kept saying; it must be untrue. Something must happen, and then everything would be in order again, the window that rattled and the patch in the linoleum. "Now then, Miss, you're only in the way without a tin hat, get along to the Centre," a fireman grumbled; but Dobbie slapped her on the shoulder; he had a list in his hand. "Was anybody there, do you know?" he inquired.

"No." Eve ran over the names in her mind. "No, I don't think so. Mr. Rashleigh didn't always come to the shelter, but tonight Miss Tippett fetched him." She had seen Angelina and Cook, Ruby of course went home to sleep, and there was Mary just in front of her. "It's a mercy it didn't hit your place," somebody said to Dobbie, and he nodded gravely.

The house that was on fire had been evacuated some weeks previously. There were a couple of minor casualties from neighbouring buildings, but nobody had been buried, and the incident, on the whole, could be considered slight. "No good looking at it, miss." Dobbie stuck the list back in his pocket. "Did you lose much?"

"No," Eve heard herself say. "Oh, no, I had sent a lot of things to my sisters in the country." That was not the point, of course; she had lost everything, but Dobbie would not understand if she tried to explain; his mind thought in items of clothes and armchairs. Nothing could ever make up to her for this robbery. The Warming Pan was a symbol of eternal freedom. She had never liked the things others loved, to find the first primrose on a freezing day or to bring back late roses to a company that would be garrulous about them year after year in exactly same words. What she wanted was the anonymous liberty of thought that her room and old Selina's cheerfulness had given her. It was less a question of atmosphere than of balance, of belief. Broad as the broadest Thames, she kept saying to herself, that was how she had seen the flowing of the years. Now all life narrowed as the bricks fell and the corner shrivelled to a point of flame and she saw herself in uniform, back in the centre of a family and a routine rigidly monotonous as school. "Better go to the Centre, miss," Dobbie tapped her shoulder again. "It will be a blow for the poor lady, she was so proud of the place. And paid her bills regular, too." Hoses were playing on the gap to try to keep the flames from spreading, and men were trampling over the bit of floor that was left. "You might tell her," Dobbie added, "that we saved the dog." And there was Beowulf, being carried up the road, his short, painted tail looking more ridiculous than ever as the flashlights caught it.

The all-clear went as Eve got to the Rest Centre door. The sky was quiet, but the streets were noisier as ambulances moved away and fresh fire engines arrived. Angelina was just in front of her, her old scarf hanging from the pocket of her leather jacket, which was now covered with thick powder from the ruins. The group from Dobbie's shelter were all in one corner of the large room, sipping mugs of tea. Lilian (really, she should be called the undaunted Lilian, Eve felt) had saved her letter case and was showing a lilac piece of paper covered with sooty fingerprints to a large audience. "Won't my niece be thrilled when she gets this, straight, as you might say, from the jaws of death!"

"They have deep shelters in Moscow," Angelina proclaimed, in a loud, accusing voice. Nobody took any notice; they were still busy trying to shake the top layer of dust from their clothes.

"I have drafted a letter to the *Times* by the light of the flares. If we had been killed in that shallow rabbit warren, the Government would have been at fault, equally with the enemy."

"Yes, dear, but would it have mattered much? To us, I mean, if we had been killed?"

"Selina, my lamb! Have you no feeling for the future? Think of posterity!"

She could not bother about anyone at the moment except herself, Miss Tippett thought, unless it were poor Mr. Rashleigh. Ferguson had gone up the road again to discover how badly the old gentleman had been hurt. The Warming Pan had gone; nobody had told her, but she felt it. It had ended its life in a blaze of glory, but she didn't want to have to look at the remains. She only wanted to sleep. "Sit down, Angelina," she suggested, "you must be tired."

"No, thank you, dear; while you have been resting— of course, I am glad that you could rest, for as far as I am concerned I shall not have a wink for a week—but while you have been resting I have made out a list of the necessary steps to take. I shall go to the Town Hall in the morning..."

"I believe you go first to Citizens' Advice," Lilian broke in, "one of my clients was bombed and that was where she went."

"I shall go, doubtless, to both. We are entitled to every assistance. After all," Angelina forgot her theories for the moment, "the enemy has destroyed our means of livelihood."

"It has gone, then—the house?"

"I'm afraid so." Ferguson tried to speak as gently as possible.

He had just returned and stood, sorrowfully, in the doorway.

"Quite gone," Selina asked in a dazed voice, "or is it ... just blitzed?" Now they had told her she could not imagine the street with no Warming Pan there.

"There was a direct hit next door and a fire. You will get compensation, you know, after the war."

"All of it has gone?" Selina remembered irrationally that square board in the top room that had always creaked. Everything had seemed so solid, so heavy.

"Absolutely, madam," Dobbie assured her in a hearty voice, his tin helmet wedged buck-fashion on his head, "but don't you fret now, it's all right, we've saved the dog."

"The dog!"

"Oh, Selina, it's a good omen, they've saved Beowulf!" Squealing joyfully, Angelina tore out into the street.

People were silent; some knew their homes were safe, others would have to wait till the morning. "Better get her a cup of tea," Dobbie whispered loudly. It was hard on an old lady like that, he thought, as he hurried back to his work outside. Selina tried to realize what it meant, but all she could see were the thick walls of the restaurant, the heavy blackout curtains. Yesterday rushed over her as if she were actually alive in it, and she started suddenly to laugh. The landlord could not send them a demand for the rent! He could never send them a demand for the rent. He could never give them notice! She laughed till the tears ran down her cheeks. She need never be frightened of the postman any more. She would not have to give Timothy or Ruby notice. The group round her looked embarrassed, and a helper tapped Ferguson on the shoulder. "Loony bin," she muttered, "but it takes some of them that way, she'll get over it. Though you'd be surprised (try one of the buns, sir, they're really quite good), some people are quite cheerful, they never say a word."

"Angelina!" Miss Tippett got up, dabbing her eyes with her handkerchief and choking: "Angelina! It's burnt! They can't send us any more bills!"

"Yes, dear, now try to be calm. They have found a Union Jack for Beowulf's collar and set him up by the big crater outside. Would you like to come and see him?"

"No," she could hardly get the words out, "no, I think I'll stay where I am." Several fellow shelterers moved round to comfort her. "Do let me wrap you up in my rug, your hands are frozen. Lilian dear, get Miss Tippett another cup of tea!" Then as she stopped laughing, they drifted away to exclaim over Beowulf. He seemed to be popular.

Ferguson sat down beside her. "I don't mind them having the bulldog or the flag," he said, looking round cautiously to see that Angelina was out of earshot, "but why both?"

"Yes, it does seem, well... the tiniest bit vulgar...." They smiled. "Still, I suppose our sense of humour is a protection. You can't imagine the Germans taking a nasty dog seriously, can you? It would shock them."

It was comfortable to have the big blanket over her shoulders. The room was warm and, apart from the voices, quiet. Some of her neighbours had settled on the floor and were trying to sleep. "Did you find out what had happened to Rashleigh?" Selina asked.

"The poor old man! The doctor told me he feared there wasn't much hope. He asked me, in fact, if I had the address of any relative. He wasn't much hurt, you know, it was merely a scratch, but his mind had gone. He kept rambling on about Indians and being scalped. Shock, I suppose."

"Yes, he was talking like that to me only . . . this evening." It seemed further away, Selina thought, than her days with Miss Humphries. "Of course, I'm not superstitious, but do you know, I had the oddest feelings getting him downstairs. The whole place smelled of death."

"Well, we hadn't been at Dobbie's ten minutes before the stuff came down. It's an exciting world." If people had listened to his warnings, Ferguson thought, none of it need have happened. "Have you anyone who will take you in tomorrow morning?"

"Yes. Mrs. Spenser will help us, I expect. My partner has been longing to take a more active part in the war than catering for ages. I am sure she will be all right. I'm not worried either about Ruby or Mary or Cook. They will soon find jobs. It's just Timothy . . . and myself," Selina said, smiling. "We're rather too old, for war."

"I know," Ferguson said, "and yet we have been part of the world. What I am trying to say is, each generation belongs in evolution; without us, there would have been something missing." Selina looked so puzzled that he hastened to add: "What people have done should be remembered as well as what they do."

"Oh, I haven't done much, I suppose; I never had the chances some of these young things get." Selina glanced at Eve, who was standing near the doorway. "But one thing I will say, I have always been willing. Oh, dear, I'll find work I know, but I shall miss my little shop. I tried to make it a home from home and to give people value for their money."

"You did, Miss Tippett, you did. You will get compensation, you know, when the war is over."

"I shall be too old then to make a fresh start."

Each looked down, away from each other, at the worn linoleum. It was true, they were not wanted. This is what came of appeasement, Ferguson thought; it was not a question of peace or war, but of good and evil. In a positive world, initiative and character counted; there was a place for everyone, but the routine that people now worshipped was a sticky trap, almost as bad as bombs. "I really believe," he said, after a long pause, "we would die rather than think."

"It was hard to realize that the Germans would be so wicked."

"People are evil, Miss Tippett, as well as unbelievably good." Had it been any other moment he would have asked her if she had ever read about the concentration camps, but tonight it would be unfair, and fortunately Dobbie came in at that moment, trying to walk quietly in his heavy rubber boots, for most of the lights had been turned out and people looked asleep, at least, under their blankets. "I wonder if you could tell me Mr. Rashleigh's next of kin? They have phoned from the hospital to say that the poor fellow died on the trip, and they want particulars."

It was inevitable, Selina supposed, but it sounded as if he were a parcel. "He had a cousin in Richmond; he made me write down the address once, in case anything happened. Would you like me to notify her?"

"It would be kind, madam, if you would drop her a note, you being the last person, as you might say, to speak with the gentleman. But I'll have to give the hospital the address, too;

they need it for the records."

"A lively night, Dobbie," Ferguson said, offering him a cigarette.

"Yes, incidents as thick as currants in a plum duff. Still, we might have had it worse here, only three fires and all under control."

"Oh, it's burnt!" Selina gave a little embarrassed giggle.

"What's burnt?"

"My address book. I remember the woman's name was Agatha, but that is not much help."

"I expect the police will trace her."

"She can't have cared much, she never came to see him."

"Well, you never know." Dobbie tried to wipe his face with an oily rag that had once been a handkerchief. "She might have felt he would be a burden, he was such a chatterer."

"I'm glad Rashleigh didn't have to suffer." It was a pity that they could not all claim a quiet, painless death when the world got tired of them. He would go on existing, Ferguson supposed; the body was tough, and would put up a doomed but desperate resistance, though the spirit was dead. He leaned forward to pick up the blanket that had slid from his knees.

"Cup of tea, sir?" One of the Rest Centre helpers came round with a tray full of mugs. It was a shock for these old men, she thought, popping an extra bit of sugar into the Colonel's tea; they ought to be in their beds, not buffeted about like this. She liked it, naturally, the easy atmosphere and the sense that every night was a picnic, but the old clung so to their possessions. "I should lie down then if I were you; everything will seem so different in the morning."

The door clattered open again and several voices said "Hush" as Angelina stumbled in, half carrying Beowulf and half bumping him on the stairs.

"Oh, dear, whatever are you doing with that plaster dog?"

"We are all made of plaster," Angelina said reprovingly.

"I'm sure I'm not!" Selina felt a good old-fashioned ague at work in her joints. "Couldn't you have left it on the pavement?"

"An idiot of a warden said somebody might trip over him and fall into the crater." She straightened the flag that was stuck in his collar. "The darling, he has brought us good luck!"

"Angelina! I am glad if that... object gives you pleasure, but as soon as you brought it into the Pan we were bombed. And now"—the realization rushed back to her—"what are we going to do with that horrible egg powder?"

"Sell it, darling, sell it at a profit in cakes. All we want is a teeny weeny oven somewhere. Leave it to me and Beowulf. If I can get wheels fitted to his dear little paws and a basket to his back, people will be tumbling over themselves to buy from me. And remember, partner, here we are alive. Why mope about the past? I'm stepping into the future...." And she slapped Beowulf so hard on the tail that a woman in the corner moaned, "Listen, they're here again, they're overhead."

"I might even get a soapbox and let him draw it."

"It's her nerves," Selina whispered; "the strain must be telling on her."

"I expect I shall have to get a hawker's licence! Won't that be fun?"

"So much depends upon one's temperament."

"Cheer up, partner, let's have a little community sing-a-long and we shall all feel better."

"Silence," somebody roared from the far end of the room, "lights out, no talking!"

Angelina shrugged her shoulders. She pushed the dog up against the wall, sat down on a mattress, and began to unlace her shoes. "As if one could sleep, at such a moment," she grumbled. Nobody wanted to be free. Stuffy fools, they wanted to sit with their silver dishes for crumpets and—why, it rhymed—their ear trumpets. She was going to tramp England, marshes, moors, heather, and gorse, she said over and over to herself; perhaps she could get a donkey as well as Beowulf. I've always wanted to be a vagabond, and I wouldn't mind, I really wouldn't mind being a weeny bit of a rogue. But she said this to herself, for Selina was being as difficult and uncooperative as possible. Taking it all tragically. But she had always been a bit of a crumpet.

Dobbie swallowed the last of his tea noisily. "See you in the morning, and don't you worry, Miss Tippett. Jerry's going to be mighty sorry for himself one day, and I hope I'm here to see it. And you did save your dog."

"Could you try to rest?" Selina looked up; she had never realized before that the Colonel was so old. He was arranging her shawl about her shoulders, and she did not mind that the shell-pink lining was covered with black smudges. "If you cared to use my flat until you can make other arrangements I should be delighted. They tell me my street is intact."

"It is really very kind of you."

"Not at all, it is a help to me to feel that I am of use."

She would never have to wake up again and worry about the rent. Only it was so strange; it wasn't two hours since she had dragged Horatio down those solid, century-old stairs. She seemed to feel the Warming Pan in her fingers, hear its creaks and noises, but it had gone, and in a little while she would be the only person to remember it. "You're wonderful," Eve said, "wonderful, but you must get out of London. Would you like to go to my sisters in the country?"

Selina shook her head. "It's silly, I suppose, but I have got to stay on here in my own village." She smiled at them both and at the nice child with the fair hair that had come round again with yet another tray.

"Have a cup of tea," her neighbour suggested, and he patted her arm.

"No, thank you, Colonel Ferguson; people are so kind, I seem to have been drinking tea all the evening. There is a war on, you know!" It was one of the stock Warming Pan jokes, and she looked up for approval. They stared back at her so seriously that she felt quite puzzled. "Oh, dear," she said, for she felt suddenly quite helpless, "I do think it is very embarrassing to be bombed."